OPAL
MOONBABY

Also by Maudie Smith

About Zooming Time, Opal Moonbaby

OPAL MOONBABY

Maudie Smith

Illustrated by Gillian Johnson

Orion
Children's Books

First published in Great Britain in 2012
by Orion Children's Books
a division of the Orion Publishing Group Ltd
Orion House
5 Upper St Martin's Lane
London WC2H 9EA
A Hachette UK Company

3 5 7 9 10 8 6 4

A catalogue record for this book is available from the British Library.

ISBN 978 1 4440 0478 6

Typeset by Input Data Services Ltd, Bridgwater, Somerset

Printed in Great Britain by Clay Ltd, St Ives plc

The Orion Publishing Group's policy is to use papers
that are natural, renewable and recyclable products
made from wood grown in sustainable forests. The logging
and manufacturing processes are expected to conform to the
environmental regulations of the country of origin.

www.orionbooks.co.uk

For Madeleine and Emma

First of all . . .

A city never sleeps but there is a time, somewhere in the early hours, long before dawn, when it grows drowsy. When parents snore their loudest and children mutter through the deepest of dreams. When slumbering dogs twitch and even the night cats let their hunting eyes close for a few precious moments.

It's only a short time, two, maybe three minutes when no one is paying attention. No one glances up at the sky and spots the revolving orb that is heading so certainly towards Archwell. No one notices it hovering over the Half Moon Estate and splitting open like an overgrown egg. No one sees the mass of sparkling particles that showers down, landing somewhere below, beneath that old copper beech tree. No one watches as the strange sphere closes again, perfectly, smoothly, as an egg can never do. Its job is done and it spins silently away out of the half light and up into the darkness, disturbing no one.

Almost no one.

Barton Green has just set out on his milk round and is meandering down Half Moon Parade. His eyes are bleary and he only has one hand on the steering wheel; there's a meat pasty in the other. He's got the radio on and he's thinking about the slice of cream cake waiting on the seat beside him.

And suddenly there she is, standing in the road, under the branches of a huge tree. A long-haired girl in a cape that is rippling with wind although the leaves on the tree are still. Her luminous hair is spinning around her head like the rotating blades of a helicopter. She's clutching something in her arms, a white creature, a cat or a small fox, and she is staring right at Barton Green with huge, gleaming violet eyes.

Barton stops thinking about cream cake and drops his pasty. He is going to hit this girl. He is going to crash right into her, he can't possibly stop in time. He cries out in horror, jumps on the brake. Too late though, surely it's too late!

The animal flies out of the girl's arms and up over the milk float but the girl doesn't move. Barton wills her to jump out of the way but she doesn't. Instead she stares straight into the headlamps and her eyes send out giant beams of blinding light. Shielding his own eyes with one arm, Barton heaves on the steering wheel. The milk float swerves, skids and thuds straight into the tree.

The sound of breaking glass seems to go on forever.

Barton jumps out and runs round to the crumpled front of the float, his heart beating hard against his chest. He is sure the girl will be lying there, crushed beneath the wheels.

She is not.

She is nowhere to be seen.

1

Martha woke up with that feeling again, the same one she had every morning. It felt as if a cold weight was pressing down on her stomach, like a stack of dinner plates. Then she remembered: school was over. It was the first day of the summer holiday and six weeks stretched ahead of her. Six whole weeks without Chloe or Colette or the rest of the Secret Circle; she wouldn't have to spend time with any of them. Martha breathed a sigh of relief.

She leaned over the side of the bunk and saw Robbie, sprawled under his jungle duvet cover, still snoring. Yoyo, his toy monkey, lay across his cheek as usual, one brown paw tucked inside Robbie's nostril.

Martha climbed down and went to the window.

'Whoops!' she exclaimed as she drew back the curtain.

'Huh? Who? Where? Whassup?' Robbie extracted Yoyo's paw from his nose. 'What's going on?'

'It's the milk float!' said Martha. 'It's crashed into a tree. There's milk and glass all over the place.'

'Cool!' Robbie hopped over to join her at the window and together they peered at the float's squashed-in bonnet. 'That float's had its chips. Do you think there are any casualties?' Casualties was Robbie's current top favourite word. He used it as often as he could. 'How about we go and see if there's any bodies?'

'How about we don't,' said Martha. 'That's not how I want to spend the first day of the holiday, thanks very much.'

'The holiday!' yelled Robbie, punching the air with his fist. 'Yessss! We can do what we like. Stay in our pyjamas and watch telly till our eyes drop out. Mum can take us swimming and maybe, just maybe, she'll *finally* take me to Pirate Planet!'

Robbie had been dying to go to the new pirate theme park ever since it had opened. He had a map of it on his wall and he could describe all the rides in minute detail. He was so obsessed with Pirate Planet, he'd even made up a song about it. He began to dance around the bedroom, singing at the top of his voice.

'Pirate Planet! Pirate Planet!
Make a date!'

Martha had heard the song thousands of times before. There wasn't much to it.

'Pirate Planet! Pirate Planet!
I can't wait!'

She put her fingers in her ears but Robbie didn't let that put him off. He just sang even louder.

'Pirate Planet! Pirate Planet!
Pirate Planet! Pirate Planet!
Pirate Planet! PIRATE PLANET!'

✰ ✲ ✳

'Pirate Planet?' said Mum, showering cereal into their bowls. 'I don't think that's on the agenda. Do you know how much those tickets cost?'

'But I've never been,' pleaded Robbie. 'I'm the only one in my class that's never been.'

'Stop exaggerating,' said Martha, seeing Mum's anxious face.

'I'm not exaggerating,' Robbie insisted. 'They've all been. Zack's been fifty million times. It's not fair!'

Mum frowned. 'Sorry, Robbie,' she said. 'But we do have to be a bit careful with money, you know.' She began to butter her toast. 'Tell you what, we'll save up for it, shall we?'

Robbie opened his mouth, ready to protest, but Martha gave him a warning look. They'd agreed not to give Mum any more worries, she had enough already. Robbie caught the look, shut his mouth, said 'Uuummpph' and began to guzzle his Space Nuggets.

'It's fine, Mum,' Martha said. 'We don't need to spend any money this holiday. We can stay at home every day if you like, just the three of us.'

Mum smiled. 'Well,' she said, waving her knife in the air, 'as a matter of fact, I've got some good news.'

'Dad's coming back!' said Robbie. 'We've won the lottery!'

'Neither of those, I'm afraid,' said Mum. 'No. I've got my old job back.'

'At Snippers?' said Martha. Snippers was the hairdressing salon in the shopping parade at the bottom of their block of flats. Mum had been a stylist there before Martha and Robbie were born.

'That's right,' said Mum. 'Only it's called A Cut Above now, since Alesha took over.'

'Very posh,' said Martha.

'Yes, and Alesha's taking me on full time. I start tomorrow. Isn't that great?'

'Cool,' said Robbie, pushing his bowl aside and spreading his toast with an extra thick layer of strawberry jam. 'I might come in one day actually, for a free haircut. You can do me an Ashley Cole, or a Matt Smith. Yeah, I want to look like Dr Who.' He picked up his monkey. 'And Yoyo fancies a quiff. What do you want, Martha?'

But Martha wasn't thinking about hairstyles. She

clutched her stomach as the stack of cold dinner plates settled in again. She had been so looking forward to staying at home with Mum this holiday, not having to worry about what anyone else was doing or saying, what anyone else thought of her. Now it looked as though Mum was planning to abandon them for the whole summer.

'What about us?' she stammered. 'Robbie and me? Will we have to go to a child minder?'

'Oh no,' said Mum, wafting the idea away. 'I can't afford one of those.'

Martha breathed a little easier.

'Thank goodness for that!' said Robbie. 'Yoyo doesn't like child minders. They're always giving him bananas when what he really wants is chocolate biscuits.'

'No,' Mum continued. 'You'll come to the salon with me. Alesha said it would be all right as long as you're well-behaved. You might even be able to help with the teas and coffees and things.'

'No way!' said Robbie. 'No way am I going to spend the entire holiday trapped in a hairdresser's!'

'Sorry,' said Mum. 'It's bad timing but the job's come up and we need the money.'

Robbie wasn't listening. 'If my friends hear about this I'm going to be a total casualty! Zack'll laugh at me!'

Martha, however, was feeling much happier. She liked the idea of helping out in the salon, passing round drinks and towels, sweeping up hair. Being tucked away in there every day would suit her right down to the ground. She'd probably never see anyone she knew, no one from school at least. It sounded just about perfect.

Robbie was shaking his head woefully and a crease had appeared between Mum's eyebrows, the one that always appeared when she was upset. Martha shot Robbie the warning look again but he wasn't receiving anything.

'I'm dead!' he said. 'I am so, so ...' Martha kicked him under the table. 'So ... ow! ... dead keen on hairdressing.' He rubbed his shin. 'Yeah, as a matter of fact I've always wanted to know about shampoo and scissors and ... and partings and stuff. Tell you what, Mum, this is probably going to be the best summer I've ever had.'

It wasn't very convincing but Martha could see Robbie was making a big effort. And it seemed to do the trick because Mum's crease disappeared like magic.

'Of course,' she said brightly. 'If it doesn't work out we'll have to think again, maybe see if one of your friends could have you to play sometimes. Perhaps you could go to Zack's house, Robbie.'

'We-ell,' said Robbie, getting into his stride. 'I suppose I might be able to spare Zack a bit of time for a game of football. As long as it's between appointments.'

Mum laughed. 'And what about you, Martha?' she said gently. 'Shall I ask Chloe's mum if she could have you occasionally?'

'No! Don't!' said Martha. The words shot out

more sharply than she had meant them to and now Mum was looking all concerned again.

'What is it with you two?' she said. 'Have you had some kind of falling out?'

'No,' said Martha. 'It's nothing. Nothing's happened. All I mean is, I'll be completely fine at the salon. I won't need to go to *anyone's* house.'

She didn't want Mum to know it but Chloe's was the last place she wanted to go.

Last summer it would have been a different story. Last summer she would have begged to go to Chloe's. Last summer she had spent almost the whole holiday with her.

Chloe had a pond in her garden and they had made a water zoo full of snails and water boatmen and mosquito larvae. They had spent hours decorating the zoo with stones and leaves and pond weed. They had even made posters advertising the place. Bramble Zoo, they'd called it. They had stuck the posters on the telegraph pole outside Chloe's house. Mum and Dad and Robbie and Chloe's family all visited the zoo and Martha and Chloe had served them bramble wine they had made themselves from blackberries mashed up with water and sugar. The wine was delicious and Martha had gone home with her mouth and her T-shirt stained a lovely purplish pink. At the end of the holiday they had sworn to reopen their zoo the following year. They had spat on their palms and shaken hands to seal the promise.

But that was almost a year ago. Before Dad had left home. Before the Secret Circle had even been invented. Long before the dreaded Colette had arrived on the estate and started at Archwell Park Primary.

Martha didn't want to see Chloe any more. She didn't even want to think about her.

For Martha had made another promise. A secret promise to herself.

She was never going to be friends with anyone ever again.

From now on she would trust no one.

No one in the entire human race.

Never ever again.

Ever.

It was a struggle to get Robbie out of bed the next morning. He wouldn't open his eyes for ages. He said they were super-glued together.

'Remember what we agreed,' said Martha, giving him a poke.

'No,' said Robbie. 'I've forgotten.'

Martha poked him again. 'We agreed to look after Mum.'

Poke.

'She's had to do absolutely everything since Dad left.'

Poke poke.

'And we've got to help her because we're all she's got, and if you don't get up now you're going to make her late for her first day at work, so get out of bed, you great big baby baboon!' She poked and tickled mercilessly until Robbie started laughing and rolled out of bed. He opened his eyes.

'All right, all right,' he groaned. 'I'll do it.' He reached for his jeans and pulled them on over his pyjamas.

'And try and sound happy about it, will you?'

In reply, Robbie gave his best grumpy baboon grunt, turned his back on her and galumphed out of the room.

He cheered up when they got outside the flats though, because the crashed milk float was still there, squashed up against the copper beech tree, surrounded by a large puddle of cheesy milk. It was being hooked up to a yellow breakdown truck, and was about to be towed away.

'What a mess!' said Mum.

Robbie ran over to have a closer look.

'That is so wicked!' he said, gazing at the smashed headlamps and the caved-in windscreen. He wrinkled his nose. 'Stinks too!'

Martha noticed a man standing nearby eating from a packet of mini scotch eggs. He was stuffing the eggs one after another into his mouth. His shoulders were hunched and he had a dazed expression on his unshaven face. She had never seen the milkman because he did his rounds before any of them were out of bed, but this man looked so unhappy she thought it must be him.

'Whoever drove into this tree must be a complete and utter idiot,' Robbie was saying in a loud voice. 'I mean it's enormous. You'd have to be a fool not to see it. You'd have to be a total numb-brain!'

The man didn't seem to notice. He just kept

swallowing his eggs and gazing up into the sky as if he expected something to fall out of it.

Martha pulled Robbie's arm. 'Come on,' she said. 'We're late.'

As they passed the tree, Martha noticed something. She couldn't quite put her finger on it. It wasn't a smell exactly and it wasn't a feeling either but there was a definite sense of something unusual in the air. It was something like spice or scent or electricity, or all three rolled into one. She didn't give it much thought at the time. But she would remember it later.

☆ ✲ ✢

'Couldn't they have come in something a bit smarter?' said Alesha, her bangles jangling from her wrists to her elbows and back again. 'This is A Cut Above, you know.'

'What's wrong with this?' asked Robbie, looking down at his Bart Simpson top which was really his pyjama top in disguise.

'Not clean for a start-off,' said Alesha, dabbing with her perfectly manicured nail at a blob of something sticky on Robbie's chest. 'Can you leave your disgusting half-chewed breakfast at home in future, please, Roberto?'

'Roberto?' Robbie looked horrified. 'That's not my name.'

'While you are in my salon, you will be Roberto,' said Alesha, who had once had a great-great-aunt who was half-Italian, and liked to pretend she was Italian herself. 'And you, Martini.' She looked at

Martha, the corners of her red mouth turned down in distaste. 'What about putting on something a little more feminine, eh? A nice skirt maybe?'

'I don't have any skirts,' said Martha.

'A dress then. You have a dress, don't you?'

Martha shook her head.

'Sorry, Alesha,' said Mum. 'I'm afraid we've got a bit of a tomboy on our hands.'

'Mamma mia!' Alesha threw up her hands dramatically. 'Trousers then. But make sure you team them with a matching tunic top or a pretty blouse. If you're going to be my little helpers you have to look good, it helps make the clients feel a bit special. Make a little effort tomorrow, OK, darling?'

Martha was squirming inside but she managed to nod. 'OK.'

Mum smiled at her reassuringly. 'We'll sort something out, won't we?'

'Well, I'm definitely not wearing a blouse,' said Robbie. 'Anyway, why do the customers—'

'Clients!' corrected Alesha.

'Why do the clients need to feel special? It's just a haircut.'

Alesha clapped her hand over his mouth. 'Oh no, Roberto,' she said. 'No, no, no. At A Cut Above there is no such thing as "just a haircut". No, we provide what I call Complete Head Refurbishments.'

Robbie sniggered into Alesha's hand. She removed it quickly.

'Is there a problemo, Roberto?' she asked. 'Something I said?'

That only made him snigger all the more.

Alesha raised her perfectly arched eyebrows. 'I hope this isn't going to be one big mistake, Mariella,' she said to Mum, whose name was actually Marie. 'To tell you the truth your kids aren't exactly what I was expecting.'

'Yes we are,' said Martha quickly. 'Or we will be. What you're expecting, I mean.' Alesha wasn't exactly what Martha had been expecting either but she was determined to make the best of things. 'What would you like us to do first?'

Alesha sniffed. 'Well, you could put the kettle on, I suppose. My first client will be arriving any secondo. The kettle's in the storeroom.' She indicated a door by the sinks.

'Right. Leave it to us,' said Martha. 'Come on, Roberto, we'll take care of the refreshments, won't we?' And before he could object, she pushed Robbie into the little room.

The first half of the morning went rather well. Martha enjoyed serving the clients with cups of tea and coffee. She helped them into the big black hairdressing capes and handed them magazines to read while they waited for Alesha or Mum to cut their hair. At the end of each Complete Head Refurbishment she brought the mirror so that they could see how they looked from the back.

Alesha was pleased with Mum's first two styles and she stopped finding fault with Martha. She even let her answer the phone once and book in an appointment. It was fun, finding a free slot in the

18

diary and writing the person's name there in pencil. 'See you next Tuesday then, at eleven thirty,' she said, just like a real receptionist.

Robbie was fine too. He was given the task of changing the CDs on the CD player and sweeping up all the hair that dropped onto the shiny floor. There was a kind of small trap door in the floor which you lifted. It had a bin underneath and you swept the hair straight into that so you didn't even have to bend down with a dustpan and pick it up. Robbie was fascinated by the secret bin under the floorboards and was kept happy swooshing all the hair into it for some time.

'You never know, Martini,' said Alesha, watching her brush a few stray hairs from a client's jacket collar. 'You carry on like this and I might even promote you to Chief Head Cleanser.'

'Chief Head Cleanser?' Martha glanced uncertainly at Mum who mouthed back, 'hair washer'.

'Oh!' said Martha, understanding. 'Oh! Thanks, Alesha. That'd be great!' Maybe they were going to make a success of this summer in the hair salon after all.

Unfortunately, the good start didn't last. In fact, it changed very quickly from a good start into a terrible one.

Martha was standing by the window, rolling up clean towels and stashing them neatly in their place on the shelf when she caught sight of a strange white object floating past outside. At first she thought it was just a stray plastic bag being blown along by the wind but then she saw that it was fluffy, like a hat or a small cushion. The odd thing was that it wasn't even windy, yet the object was somersaulting along at quite a speed. It looked to Martha as if it was self-propelled, as if it had a life of its own. At one point it did a sort of nose dive and Martha stepped back, afraid it was going to smash right into the window, but then it veered off at the last second and flitted easily away. Martha thought she saw something glinting on it too, like a scrap of blue tinsel.

'Look at that!' she cried, as the object drifted out of sight. At the same moment, Robbie, who had obviously seen it too, ran forwards, hoping to get a better look, but he had forgotten to put the lid on the trap door. He put his foot straight in it, tripped and banged hard into Alesha, who stumbled and cut a huge jagged chunk out of her client's long hair.

'Caramba!' screamed Alesha.

'My hair!' wailed the client. 'What have you done to my lovely hair?'

'Sorry,' said Robbie. 'I didn't mean to.'

'Shut up! Idiot!' Alesha hissed. Then she made her voice go all soft and soothing. 'Don't worry, madam, I can sort it. I'll do you something really magnifico. Something to die for!'

'You know what,' said Robbie, trying to be helpful, 'it looks quite good jagged. Maybe you should do the rest like that. It's quite sci-fi actually.'

'Sci-fi?' screeched the client. '*Sci-fi?* I'm going to a wedding, *my* wedding, on Saturday, not a science fiction convention. What's my fiancé going to say

when I turn up at the registry office looking like some
. . . some mad Martian? What am I going to say to him?'

'I come in peace?' suggested Robbie.

The client burst into tears.

'That's it!' said Alesha, brandishing her scissors
menacingly. 'Mariella! Get this boy out of here before
I chop him into little pieces!'

Mum sighed and slowly put down her scissors and
comb, as if for the last time. She went to get their
jackets from the coat stand.

'I'm sorry, Alesha,' she said. 'I suppose I should have
realised it couldn't really work with all of us here.'

'It's all right, Mum,' said Martha, rushing up and
taking her own and Robbie's jackets from her. 'It can
work. It will! You carry on.' She couldn't let Mum
give up that easily. 'Let me take Robbie outside to
the play area,' she said. 'We can take our sandwiches.
We'll be fine out there, honestly. We'll stay right
where you can see us. Then you can carry on with
your hairdressing.' She pointed to the client who was
waiting patiently in Mum's chair, her glossy hair
almost completely blow-dried into perfect shape.
'You're really good at it, Mum. Please stay.'

Mum looked at Alesha, who shrugged. 'Just so
long as your kids aren't under my feet any longer.'

'Thanks, Alesha,' said Mum, hanging her coat
back up. 'Thanks for being so understanding.'

'Yes, well,' said Alesha, handing her sniffling client
a box of tissues. 'As long as you realise, Mariella, if
there's one more slip like this, one tiny little slip, it'll
be finito for you too. And I'm not kidding.'

'I really, really wish that hadn't just happened,' said Martha. They were sitting on top of the concrete pipe in the play area staring out over Archwell Park, munching sausage sandwiches.

'Me too,' said Robbie. 'I thought I was a casualty there for a minute. Did you see the way Alesha came at me with those scissors? She was scary, like Cruella de Vil on a bad hair day.'

'Well, you can't blame her for being angry. You did wreck her client's hairdo.'

The door of A Cut Above opened and Martha put a warning hand on Robbie's wrist, nodding towards the person who was coming out. They watched as the client with the newly jagged haircut set off up the street, still wiping her eyes on a damp wad of Alesha's pastel-coloured tissues. Martha and Robbie sat very still until she was safely round the corner.

'It wasn't my fault,' said Robbie as soon as she disappeared from view. 'It was that flying thing. It put me off.'

'I know,' said Martha. 'What *was* that thing, do you think?'

'Baby swan, I reckon,' said Robbie. 'Come to check out the paddling pool, see if it could find another swan to be its mate.' He nodded towards the concrete paddling pool that was fenced off at the end of the play area. 'Hey! Shall we go for a paddle?'

'No,' said Martha. 'We've got to stay here. You do realise we could have lost Mum her job just then? I don't know what's going to happen now. Alesha won't let us help in the salon, that's for sure.'

'Good,' said Robbie, through a mouthful of sausage. 'That means Mum'll have to ask Zack's mum to look after me. I'd much rather go to Zack's house, even if he is going to boast about all the things he's doing this summer.' He kicked his feet against the hard pipe. 'Trouble is, Zack's surfing in Cornwall this week. Maybe next week I can though.'

'Well that's fine for you,' said Martha. 'But I don't want to go to Chloe's, this week or next week.'

'So what's new? You never want to go to Chloe's any more. I don't know what's wrong with her so suddenly.'

'You wouldn't understand,' said Martha.

'Yes I would. I understand everything. Tell me anything you like and I'll understand it immediately. Go on, try me.'

'Thanks,' said Martha. 'But no thanks.'

It was tempting to tell someone how she felt but she couldn't trust Robbie. Even if she made him promise not to, he would be bound to go and tell Mum, and Martha didn't want to give Mum anything else to worry about. She'd been so sad since Dad had left home and now she was trying really hard to keep this job. The best thing was to keep Mum well out of it.

'Is it 'cos Chloe's gone off with that new girl? The one with the pointy shoes and the snorty laugh?'

'No,' said Martha. 'It's got nothing to do with Colette.'

'Bet it has,' said Robbie.

'It hasn't. And I'm not going to tell you about it, so stop fishing!'

But it did have something to do with Colette. It had everything to do with Colette. Since the day she'd arrived at school and Chloe had invited her to join the Secret Circle, things had gone badly downhill for Martha.

The Secret Circle was a club. It had been a very small club to begin with. It had a membership of only two: Martha and Chloe. Chloe was Club President and so was Martha. Martha was Club Secretary and so was Chloe. They shared everything. The club was responsible for searching for lost animals, spying on bad people, writing stories, and making up new games – all the things that Martha and Chloe loved to do together. They made special membership badges, which they wore secretly inside their coats. It had been wonderful having a club that no one else belonged to or even knew about. It was just the two of them.

Then Colette had arrived on the Half Moon Estate. She and her dad moved into the caretaker's bungalow. Soon afterwards she turned up at school with her pierced ears and her trendy little skirts.

Everyone was intrigued by the new girl. At break time, they all hovered about her, like wasps round a jar of jam, while she told stories about her old school, which was apparently much bigger than Archwell Park Primary, and about London, where she had moved from. She didn't call it London though. She called it 'the capital'. Everyone was so impressed. It was only her first day, and Chloe, without even asking Martha, came straight out and invited Colette to join the Secret Circle. Martha couldn't believe it. She, for one, was not impressed by Colette. Quite the opposite. There was something about Colette's wide smile that made Martha feel uncomfortable. She had a harsh, loud laugh that made you jump, even if you knew it was coming. And she never seemed to be laughing with you, it was always at you. Colette laughed a lot.

She joined the Secret Circle at once and quickly took over. She became President and Secretary too and she invited more girls to join. Soon the club wasn't about animals and games; Colette said all that was for babies. Now it was about fashion, shopping and make-up. Martha wasn't interested in fashion; she liked jeans and T-shirts and stuff that didn't get in the way. She hated going in big shops, they made her feel sick. She had tried on some make-up once but her cheeks came out in a rash that lasted for days. She appealed to Chloe to get rid of Colette and return the club to how it was at the beginning. How it was meant to be. But Chloe seemed to like all the new ideas. She began to dress like Colette, wearing tight black skirts it was impossible to run in, trying out different make-up and jewellery. She spent less and less time with Martha, and more and more with Colette. If Martha asked Chloe to come over to her flat after school, somehow Colette was always there at Chloe's shoulder, giving her a hug and saying, 'Oh no, Chlo, you can't. You're coming to mine. We're going to do our nails, remember? You promised.' Or, 'Oh sorry, Martha, Chloe's coming to town with me after school. We're going to buy ourselves a braiding set.'

And then the worst day of all. Colette came in with new membership badges for the Secret Circle. She said the original ones, which Martha had designed in the shape of clover leaves with ladybirds on, were too babyish. She had made new ones, black circles with glittery gold stars. She handed them out at playtime. Martha had hoped that someone, Chloe maybe, would stand up for the old badges, but no one did. On Colette's orders, they all tore the clover leaves from the insides of their jackets and put them in the school bin with the rotten banana skins and old snack wrappers. Martha pretended to do the same but when she thought no one was looking she tucked her badge away in her pocket. She planned to take it home and put it in the cardboard box under her bed with her other treasures.

They were heading back up the stairs to class when Martha found Colette standing in front of her, blocking her path.

'Martha Stephens,' said Colette, looking down at her from a higher step. 'You have just failed the Secret Circle Trust Test!'

'What Trust Test?' said Martha. 'What are you talking about?'

'I'm talking,' said Colette, placing her hands on her hips, 'about your old membership badge. You know it's expired. But you didn't throw it away, did you?'

'I wanted to keep it. So what?'

'So what? You've only broken a golden rule of the Secret Circle, that's all. You've let everyone down. The whole club!'

'No I haven't.' Martha glanced at the other girls, who were clustering around Colette. 'You don't mind if I keep my old badge, do you? I mean, what does it matter?'

No one answered. No one met her gaze.

'It matters a lot,' said Colette. 'To be honest, Martha, this is the last straw.' She sighed loudly. 'Now don't imagine that we haven't given this loads of thought, because we have. Loads.'

Martha was baffled. 'What are you going on about, Colette? I don't understand.'

Colette shook her head sadly. 'No, you don't, do you? You hardly ever do. I'm afraid it's just not working out, Martha.'

'What isn't?'

'You and the Secret Circle. You see, the fact is I just don't think you're suited to it.'

'Of course I'm suited to it. I half invented it!'

'Yes,' said Colette, her voice hardening now. 'But things have moved on since then. We're not messing about in ponds now, playing with teddies and stuff, we're not a little kids' playgroup. We're a proper girls' club, addressing proper, serious issues.'

'What?' said Martha, 'Like how to attach false fingernails? Or ten things to say to get a boy to like you? Or what to wear to a disco? What's so serious about all that?'

Colette pursed her lips. 'This is exactly the kind of behaviour we were talking about, isn't it, Chlo?' Chloe nodded and looked away before Martha could catch her eye. Colette went on, 'I may as well get to the point, Martha. The thing is, we don't want you in the Secret Circle any more. We're cancelling your membership.' She held out her hand. 'Your badge, please!'

Martha was astounded. Tears pricked her eyes and threatened to fall down her cheeks. Angrily she tore off the new badge and slapped it onto Colette's waiting palm.

'Have your stupid badge. I hate it anyway. And I don't want to be in the Secret Circle any more either. You can keep it!'

Colette smirked. 'The Secret Circle's going to be the best club in the world from now on. Let's go, guys.' She closed her hand over the badge, turned on her heel and trotted up to class. Chloe and the other girls followed her, leaving Martha on her own at the foot of the stairs.

It was the worst moment of her life. How she had managed to climb the mountain to the classroom she never knew. She had gone in and sat down in her usual seat, the one next to Chloe's. Chloe had turned her chair away and was huddling together with Colette and the others, whispering. All Martha had to look at was Chloe's plait that hung down her back and was threaded with the beads that Colette had chosen for her from their new braiding set.

Martha had to keep rubbing her eyes and when the teacher asked if something was wrong she said she thought a fly must have flown into her eye. There had been no fly, of course, and the others all knew that. Still, no one had said anything nice to her. No one had tried to comfort her. She was on her own. And it had stayed like that for the rest of the term. Even now when she thought about it a terrible ache surged through her stomach, making her want to be sick.

'Martha!' Robbie was saying, 'Martha, are you listening to me? There's a wombat in the pipe!'

'What?' Martha shook off the horrible memory and snapped back into the present. 'What did you say?'

Robbie started sneezing wildly. '*Achoo!* There's a w-*achoo*! Wombat! It's underneath us in the pipe. I just saw it. It popped out. *Achoo!*'

'It can't be. We don't have wombats in this country.'

'Well it looked like a wombat to me. I saw one on *Katie Crumble's Cutest Critters*. Anyway, whatever it

30

is, it's making my *achoo!* nose tickle. *Achoo!* I can't stop sn-*achoo*-zing!' He pinched his nose between his finger and thumb. 'I mean sneezing.'

Martha leaned over the rim of the pipe and peered inside. Sure enough, there was an animal in there. A white fluffy animal with large round amber eyes, sharply pointed ears and a tiny pink nose. It didn't look like a cat exactly, or a dog, or even a fox. It certainly wasn't a wombat.

'Hello,' said Martha to the animal. 'Who are you then?'

As if to answer her, the animal made a series of little rumbling and chattering sounds. Then it darted out of the pipe and scampered towards an open door on the ground floor of the flats. Before it reached the door it turned and chattered again.

Robbie pulled up his pyjama top and blew his nose on Bart Simpson. 'Look,' he said. 'It wants us to follow it.' He slid down off the pipe and headed after the creature, which was about to go into the flats.

'Wait!' said Martha. 'We can't. We promised we'd stay here.' She could see Mum through the salon window, showing another client into her chair. Mum saw her too and smiled and gave her the thumbs-up. Martha gave her the thumbs-up back.

'Come on,' said Robbie. 'Quick! I think it's lost.'

Martha knew they shouldn't go into the flats on their own. The flats on the ground floor were empty and being redecorated for the next tenants. They were definitely out of bounds. Colette's dad, who was the caretaker now, had put up a KEEP OUT sign. But Robbie was right, the animal could be lost. And it would be something to do while Mum was cutting hair. It might even keep Robbie out of trouble.

'OK,' Martha said, looking back at Mum who was now concentrating on combing out her new client's curly hair. 'We'll go after it. But only for a minute. Then we come straight back here.'

They ran after the animal as it disappeared into the flats. For a moment they lost sight of it but then it appeared at the end of the darkened corridor. It was sitting up on its hind legs, almost as if it was waiting for them. As they came closer Martha noticed that it had orange stripes and spots on its white underbelly. It was a very unusual creature. They had almost caught up with it when it ran off again, faster than before. It skittered over the polished floors so fast Martha could have sworn she saw blue sparks flying from its tail. She was about to ask Robbie whether he saw them too when the animal ground to a halt and bounded into an open doorway.

Martha and Robbie hesitated at the door. It didn't seem right to go into the flat, and there was a strange smell emanating from it, like sparklers and hot pepper. Martha realised she had smelled that same smell before. It had been floating around near the copper beech tree outside their flat, and by the crashed milk float. It wasn't a normal sort of smell at all.

They were beginning to back away when a cheery voice called, 'About zooming time! I thought you were never zooming coming!'

4

A girl stood in the doorway. A most extraordinary girl. She was tall and thin as a stick insect and had long pale hands. She was wearing a big purple shirt and flared purple trousers with a silver belt and silver boots. Round her neck was a chunky necklace made with lumps of brightly coloured glass. Her hair, which was silvery white, stuck out in all directions as if she had just rubbed a balloon over it. And her eyes were like no eyes Martha had ever seen. They were deep mauve, like violets, and the pupils at their centres were not black like most people's, but sapphire blue and sparkling. She was grinning from one pointed ear to the other and displaying a jumbled set of exceedingly white teeth.

The fluffy creature was in the girl's arms and licking her face all over, as if it thought she was its baby and needed a good wash. The girl was stroking

the animal and it was making a rumbling noise which sounded like purring or maybe scolding, Martha couldn't tell which.

The girl bowed. 'Opal Moonbaby the fourteenth!' she announced. 'Delighted to make your acquaintances!'

Robbie and Martha stared at her, open-mouthed.

'Isn't it your turn to introduce yourselves now?' she asked. 'Or have I got this whole manners thing wrapped round my knee?'

Martha closed her mouth. 'Sorry,' she mumbled, trying not to stare quite so much. 'I'm Martha.'

'Robbie,' said Robbie. 'Pleased to mee – *achoo* – meet you. Is that *your* wombat?' he asked, letting out a stream of six more sneezes.

'Ah yes,' said the girl. 'I didn't quite finish the introductions, did I? How rude!' The animal had finished washing her face now and was nuzzling her with its nose. The girl nuzzled it back. 'It's all right, Garnie,' Martha heard her whisper. 'I'm fine. I had my eye on you the whole time and I'm absolutely tickety boop.'

She held the animal up for them to see. 'This is Garnet. He is not, however, a wombat. He is my constant companion and I depend upon him wholly and completely entirely. Give them a swirl, Garnet.'

In response, Garnet turned his head as if to show himself off. But he didn't turn his head to the right and then to the left in the way another animal might, he twirled it all the way round.

35

'Wow!' exclaimed Robbie. 'A three-sixty! I nearly did one of those once, on Zack's skateboard, but I've never seen anyone do one with their head before. What is he – *achoo* – exactly? Is he some kind of big – *achoo* – guinea pig? I'm allergic to guinea pigs.'

'Allergic?' said Opal Moonbaby. 'What's that?'

Before they could answer she said, 'Hold your houses, I'll look it up.'

She began to blink very rapidly. She did this for a few seconds and then opened her eyes wide. 'Got it!' she declared. '*Allergy: hypersensitivity, disorder of the immune system.*' She smiled. 'Clear as muck!'

'Mud,' corrected Martha.

'What?' said Opal.

'Mud,' repeated Martha. 'That's how the saying goes – it's clear as mud, not muck.'

'If you say so,' answered Opal, in a way that suggested she didn't think this information was either important or interesting.

'Yes, you can stroke him if you like,' she said to Robbie, who hadn't said anything but in fact wanted nothing more than to stroke Garnet, even though he was making his eyes red and itchy. He went over, wiping his runny nose on his sleeve.

Martha remained standing in the doorway. She wasn't at all sure whether to go in. The flat was completely empty. There was no furniture in it whatsoever. There weren't even any curtains up. And there was something very odd about this girl. What was she doing here? Had she broken in? Was she part of a gang of criminals? Could she be dangerous?

'I'm not a burglar,' said Opal, as if she had been reading Martha's thoughts. 'There has been no breaking and entering, no unlawful removal of property or any such stuff. I'm simply borrowing this accommodation for a short time.'

'Do you mean you're a squatter?' said Martha. She'd heard about squatters on the news, how they took over empty houses and lived in them without paying any rent.

'Sure am!' said Opal. 'I can squat with the best of them. Here, look!' She began to perform a series of squats. Then she folded her arms and bobbed up and down, thrusting out her legs one at a time, like a Russian dancer.

'Not that kind of squatter,' said Martha.

Opal got to her feet and blinked her eyes ten times very fast. 'Oh,' she said. 'See what you mean. You think I'm crouching on someone else's land. Well I suppose you could call it crouching. I prefer to call it caretaking. I'm just taking care of this flat for a little while, that's all.'

'These flats have already got a caretaker,' said Martha. 'So you must be a croucher ... I mean a squatter.' Martha wasn't sure if squatters were good or bad. She guessed they were probably a lot better than burglars. Opal didn't actually look bad. She just looked a bit strange.

Robbie was sneezing uncontrollably now, all over Garnet and Opal.

'This allergy lark is no fun at all, is it?' said Opal cheerfully, brushing droplets of mucus from her arms.

'Darn it, Garnet! Can't you vamoose out of the way so this boy can be a bit less sneezy?'

Then something wonderful happened. The fluffy creature that was lying so contentedly in Opal Moonbaby's arms suddenly produced webbed wings, like a bat's, and flapped up into the air. It glided across the room and landed on the windowsill. It folded the wings against its body and settled down for a nap in the sunshine.

'How's that?' said Opal, looking pleased with herself.

'Amazing!' said Robbie, his mouth hanging open. 'Magic!'

'What kind of animal is he?' asked Martha in astonishment. She had an encyclopaedia of animals from all over the world, but there was nothing quite like this in there.

'Garnet is a mingle,' announced Opal. 'He is several animals rolled into one. All their best bits have been mingled and merged together. He has the eyes of an owl, the ears and tail of a lynx, the fur of a Persian cat, the wings of a flying fox, the nostrils of a stoat and the intelligence of a pot-bellied pig. Quite a combination, don't you think?'

'But how is that possible?' asked Robbie.

'It isn't,' said Martha. 'It's ridiculous.'

It was a wild and wonderful idea but it was totally mad. The girl had to be making it up.

'I'm not making it up,' Opal said. 'I merged him myself. I selected all my favourite animal elements from the Mingle Manual, keyed them into the

Minmangulator and five minutes later out he popped. He really is quite the cutest and most splendid mingle I ever managed.' She hopped up onto the windowsill next to Garnet and stroked his head. Immediately he began a loud rumbling purr.

'You're a witch,' said Robbie, impressed. 'You must be. You're a witch, aren't you?'

Opal laughed. She threw back her head and yelped with laughter. She slapped her thighs and laughed some more. She laughed until tears sprang into her amethyst eyes. Then she stopped.

''Course I'm not a witch. I'm a Carnelian.'

'What's a Carnelian?' asked Robbie.

'Someone who comes from Carnelia, obviously,' said Opal. 'There's lots of us there, the Starsons, the Comets, the Asteroys. Oh, and the Mercurials, of course.' She wrinkled her nose. 'I can't forget those crawly creepies, more's the shame. The Moonbabies are the most important family though. You don't need to worry about any of those other clans.'

'Carnelia,' said Martha doubtfully. 'Is that a country?' She had quite a good grasp of geography but she had never heard of a country called Carnelia.

Opal sighed as if she had just realised she was dealing with dimwits. 'Of course it's not a country,' she said. 'Carnelia, as everyone knows, is a planet!'

'Do you mean you're an alien?' asked Robbie, his jaw dropping several centimetres.

'An alien?' said Opal. 'I don't know. Let me see.' She did that flickering thing with her eyes again.

Martha had never seen anyone's eyelids flutter so quickly. They went incredibly fast, like the pages of a book when you flick through them without reading any of the words.

'Oh!' said Opal, opening her eyes wide. 'You mean *a creature from another world*. That kind of alien. Well, I suppose I must be, since I certainly don't belong here on Earth. Thank goodness! It's a real dump, don't you think?'

'Yeah, it is a bit of a dump,' Robbie agreed. 'Especially Archwell. By the way, why do you do that funny thing with your eyes?'

'I only learned your language last week,' Opal explained. 'So I still have to look up the odd word. I've got an English dictionary implant in one of my spare brain pockets. Very footy.'

'I think you mean handy,' said Robbie, giggling.

'Probably,' said Opal.

'Can I ask a question?' said Robbie. He didn't seem to realise he'd already asked several.

Opal Moonbaby didn't mind. 'Shoot away,' she said.

'If your name's Moonbaby, shouldn't you come from the Moon?'

'The first ever Moonbabies lived on the Moon.'

Now Martha knew Opal was lying. No one had ever lived on the Moon. It was impossible. She knew that for a fact.

'Not your Moon, Martha,' said Opal. 'The Moonbabies came from the Carnelian Moon. They all moved to Carnelia about six thousand eons ago.

I've only been to the Carnelian Moon once myself, when I went crater diving.'

'Crater diving! Whoa!' Robbie's mouth hung open in admiration. Martha could see he was completely taken in by this girl. But *she* wasn't going to be so easy to fool. Aliens? Brain pockets? A planet called Carnelia? Really! She must think they were born yesterday.

'Actually,' said Opal, with an extra innocent smile, 'you were born on the eighteenth of your October, precisely nine years, eight months, twenty-four days, five hours and forty-three seconds ago. Not yesterday at all.'

Martha looked at her watch and did a quick sum in her head. Opal had everything perfectly correct, her birth date, her age, even the time of her birth, half past seven in the morning. Mum had told her that she was born in a great hurry just before breakfast. She felt both shocked and annoyed that Opal could be so accurate.

'What are you? Some kind of mind reader?'

'I do tune in to the occasional brain frequency, yes, since you ask,' answered Opal carelessly.

'Well, don't!' said Martha crossly. 'Thoughts are private, you know!'

'Not on Carnelia, they're not.'

'Well they are on Earth, so cut it out!'

'Sorry,' said Opal, 'I'll stop it at once. I give you my solemn Carnelian promise. I hate to upset a friend.'

'I'm not your friend,' said Martha.

'Not yet perhaps.'

'Not ever!'

'Hatty tatty!' said Opal, making a face.

'It's hoity toity!'

Martha grimaced. What she had just said made it sound as if she half-believed the girl's story about being a mind reader and coming from a planet called Carnelia. And she definitely didn't believe it. Not for a minute.

'I'll be your friend,' Robbie piped up. 'I'd love to be your friend.' He couldn't think of anything more exciting than having an alien for a friend. An alien with a flying pet. An alien who could read people's minds, had purple eyes and an entire dictionary stuffed in her head. It was fantastic. Just wait till he told Zack!

Opal was studying him carefully. 'Of course, you do realise that you mustn't tell anyone about me,' she said. 'If word gets out, I'll be a celebrity in no time. I'll be plastered all over the internet before you can say Jack Higginson. We can't have that, or I'll fail the challenge.'

'What challenge?' asked Robbie.

'It's nothing really,' said Opal. 'Just a regular three-part challenge we Carnelians have to do from time to time. Number One: I have to spend a month living as a human being. Well, there's not much to that, is there? Should be as easy as falling off a dog. Number Two: I have to make sure I don't get famous. No pictures in the paper or anything like that. And Num—' She suddenly shut her mouth as if she had caught a fly in it. Then she opened it again and said, 'And that's it. Should be a doodle. I'll have my CIA in no time.'

'CIA?' asked Robbie.

'Carnelian Independence Award,' said Opal. 'It's proof that you've learned to survive on other planets. Could be useful if Carnelia ever blows up or implodes or anything.'

'Do you mean Carnelians have been here before, and no one even knew about them?' Robbie asked.

'Not if they were doing their job properly, they didn't,' said Opal. 'Anyway, I don't suppose many of them came to Earth, it's such a backward type of planet. No swimbats or fantariums. Not a single sledspangle in sight! What *do* you all do for fun?'

'We probably haven't got anything as good as fantariums,' said Robbie, 'Whatever *they* are. But we've got swimming pools and flume slides. There's skateboarding and computer games and crazy golf. And I bet you'd have a great time at Pirate Planet! It's so cool!'

'Pirate Planet, eh?' said Opal. 'Well, I'll fly anything once.'

Martha was getting annoyed again. 'Say you really are an alien,' she said. 'Which I'm sure you're not. Why did you choose Earth for your challenge, if it's so backward? And what's the third part?'

'Mm?' murmured Opal, concentrating on a speck of something invisible on her shirt.

'You said it was a three-part challenge, but you only mentioned two things. What's the third?'

43

Opal glanced sideways at Martha through silvery lashes. 'Did I really say three parts? Silly old me! No, it's only two parts. Part One and Part Two. That's all.'

Martha wasn't convinced. 'I've had enough of this,' she said. 'Come on, Robbie. We're going.'

'Don't go now,' Opal said. 'Not when we're just getting to know each other.'

'Can't we stay a bit longer?' Robbie pleaded.

'No! We've been away too long already. Mum might have missed us.'

'Same time tomorrow then, friends,' said Opal briskly. 'You can help me fix this place up a bit, take me shopping, throw me the ropes. '

'We're not your friends and we won't be coming back tomorrow,' Martha said, in as withering a tone as she could muster.

'The next day then,' said Opal.

'No.'

'Day after that?'

'Never. Not in one billion light-years.'

She closed the door firmly in Opal's dismayed face. Of course they wouldn't be going back tomorrow. They couldn't go even if they wanted to. And she certainly didn't want to. Friends indeed! She had sworn never to make friends with anyone again. And there was no way she was going to make an exception for this so-called alien. Opal Moonbaby could find someone else to be her friend because Martha definitely wasn't interested.

5

Martha and Robbie were back in their place on the concrete pipe when Mum came out to fetch them. She took them back into A Cut Above where they both apologised to Alesha and promised never to cause any more accidents. They still had to spend the rest of the day sitting in the cramped storeroom of the salon. Alesha said it was the only way. She had had to give the long-haired client who was getting married a free Head Refurbishment and the promise of a discount if she ever came back, which Alesha seriously doubted she would. So thanks to them, Alesha said, she was losing money rather than making it. She seemed to be very pleased with Mum's haircutting though, and said that she could stay on as a stylist, but only if Martha and Robbie remained in the storeroom and kept as quiet as 'little tiny mousettos'.

Robbie sat on a stack of cardboard boxes and talked non-stop about Opal Moonbaby. He wanted to tell Mum about her but Martha reminded him that if they did that, Mum would also find out that they had been inside the empty flats and then they would be in big trouble.

'Anyway,' she said, from her perch on the counter, 'I don't know why you're so interested in her. She's probably making all that stuff up. There's no way she's an alien. It's just a load of rubbish.'

'Oh no,' said Robbie. 'She's an alien all right. She's so funny looking. I mean she's not green or anything like you'd expect but she's got that hair and those weird eyes and she smells funny. You saw her doing that mad dictionary thing with her eyes. She's even got brain pockets!'

'Well if you believe that you'll believe anything,' said Martha. 'I don't think she's an alien at all. More like some kind of con artist.'

'Well, how come she knew your exact age, down to the last second? How could she know a thing like that?'

'Lucky guess,' said Martha, not very convincingly.

'All right,' said Robbie. 'You obviously don't want to believe in her. But I do. I think she's awesome. And there's one thing even you can't explain.'

'What?'

'Garnet!' said Robbie triumphantly. 'His revolving head, and the blue sparks we saw. And the wings? How do you explain his wings?'

Martha thought for a moment. 'I don't know,' she

said. 'He's probably just some new species we haven't heard of yet, that's all.'

Robbie snorted. 'Oh yeah! Like that wouldn't have been in the news! A flying fox-owl-cat-dog-pig! We'd definitely have heard of that if it existed on Earth.'

'Maybe I can't explain it,' said Martha. 'But that doesn't mean there isn't an explanation. There must be. All I know is we shouldn't get involved. That girl gives me a funny feeling. We should stay out of her way.'

But staying out of Opal Moonbaby's way wasn't going to be easy. Opal would see to that.

✳ ✳ ✳

The next morning, no sooner had Alesha marched them into the storeroom and firmly closed the door on them, than Opal appeared on top of the concrete pipe outside. She was wearing a purple cape, sunglasses and a floppy hat and she was jumping up and down and waving. She looked ridiculous.

Robbie waved back through the window. Martha didn't wave. She turned away and opened her bag. She had brought whole families of badgers and hedgehogs from her old animal collection to help pass the time. She began to arrange them on a box in front of her, but all the time her ears were drawn to the very loud conversation that Robbie was trying to conduct with Opal Moonbaby.

'Yes it is a lovely day, isn't it?' he called. 'How's

Garnet? What did you say? He's banished? Where's he been banished to?'

There was a pause, then Robbie bellowed, 'Oh! *Famished*! Sorry, thought you said *banished*. What? You're famished too? Oh, right.' He turned to Martha. 'What's famished mean?'

'Hungry, I think,' said Martha. 'Can you be a bit quieter?'

Robbie ignored her and began to shout. 'Sorry you're hungry. You can have some of my packed lunch if you like.' Opal said something and then Robbie yelled even louder, 'I SAID YOU CAN HAVE SOME OF MY SANDWICHES IF YOU LIKE! DO YOU WANT PEANUT BUTTER AND SALAMI OR CHOCOLATE SPREAD WITH CUCUM ...'

'What is this gigantico racket?' Alesha burst in, brandishing her comb. 'I can't hear myself think out there. Artists like me, you know, we're very sensitivo. We can't be expected to work in these conditions.'

'Sorry,' said Martha, glaring at Robbie. 'We'll be quiet from now on, I promise.'

'Too late for that, bambinos!' said Alesha. 'The damage is done. Outside! You can do your shouting on the swings. I can't cope with you in here, you're doing my head in.'

So to Robbie's delight and Martha's dismay, they were sent straight out into the play area where Opal Moonbaby was waiting for them.

She was hopping along the old drainpipe like a big

purple flamingo. When she saw them approaching she hopped down at once, landing on one silver boot.

'Thank my mucky stars, you're here!' she said, grinning at them from behind her sunglasses. 'Silliest thing's happened. I forgot to bring a proper supply of scoff capsules with me and now I'm absolutely starving hungry.'

'What are scoff capsules?' said Robbie.

'They're capsules you scoff, of course,' said Opal, 'to ward off hunger twangs. I should have had at least three by this time of day but I haven't had a single one.' She took hold of her stomach and shook it with both hands. 'See,' she said. 'Totally empty jelly. Garnet's the same. I forgot his scoff capsules too.'

Garnet's head appeared from Opal's cape pocket. He looked at them with large doleful eyes and gave a pathetic whimper, as if to confirm that his belly too was totally empty.

'I really ought to look after him better,' said Opal, giving Garnet a comforting scratch under the chin. 'I'd die if anything happened to Garnie.'

'I feel the same way about Yoyo,' said Robbie, taking the well-worn monkey out of his pocket.

'Yes,' said Opal, 'you do. But the difference is that I really would die. Carnelians can't survive on other planets without their mingles. They fade away to nothing. So it's vital that I take extra special care of him while we're here.'

'What do you expect us to do about it?' said Martha.

'Help me get some food, of course. Take me to

your Earth shop. Find me some provisions.'

'No way!' said Martha. 'We can't just leave and go to the shops. Our mum would kill us.'

'What?' said Opal. 'Kill you? Would she really? Just for helping someone get a bit of nourishment? That's a bit zooming harsh, isn't it?'

'No,' answered Martha, trying to be patient. 'I don't mean she'd actually kill us. I mean – oh, never mind! The point is we can't help you. Sorry, but this is your problem, not ours.'

'Oh, I see.' Opal looked crestfallen. 'It's because we're not friends yet, isn't it?'

'Something like that,' said Martha. The three of them fell silent and the silence was filled by an enormous gurgle in Opal's stomach.

'We could go to the new mini-market,' said Robbie. 'It's just round the corner. It would only take a few minutes.'

Opal brightened up at this. 'Could we?' she said. 'That would be so fantastically brilliantly splendidly awesome!' She ran up the slide, threw herself on her back and slid down and right off the end. She lay on the bark chips, staring up at Martha. 'Could we, Martha? Could we really go to the mini-market together?'

'Go on, Martha,' said Robbie. 'Mum won't miss us.'

Martha was just about to say no, they absolutely couldn't go to the mini-market, when she caught sight of Chloe and Colette sauntering towards the play area. Colette had her arm hooked through

Chloe's and she was whispering and giggling into her ear. It looked like they were heading straight for the swings, straight for where Martha was standing.

'All right,' she said. 'But we'll have to be quick.' She turned and strode purposefully towards the road, Robbie and Opal skipping along behind her.

As they passed the large glass window of A Cut Above, Martha and Robbie kept Opal between them and the salon. If Mum did happen to look out she would only see Opal in her big purple cape and not notice Martha and Robbie sneaking along next to her.

Opal lifted her sunglasses and peered into the salon window. 'It's all right,' she said. 'She's in the back room drinking something hot and red, and looking through a giant book of hairstyles. Oh yes, and she's scratching a pimple under her eyebrow.'

'That'll be her rosehip tea she's drinking. It's her favourite. How can you see all that from here?' said Robbie, straining to see anything inside the salon at all.

'She can't,' said Martha. 'She's making it up to impress you.'

'Not a bit of it,' said Opal. 'My eyes are my strength. Everyone who lives on Carnelia has a special strength somewhere, in their ears or their noses or even their teeth. The Mercurials have power in their hair, and the Starsons have it in their toes. You don't want to know where the Asteroys have theirs!' Opal chuckled to herself.

'You can have power in any bit of your body,' she

went on. 'But we Moonbabies have power in our eyes and that's the best power there is. I can see what people are thinking. I can see through things and I can see a really long way. For example, I can tell you that the weather is very nice in France just at the moment, but there's a big cloud on its way from Italy so those Frenchies had better make the most of it.'

'Rubbish,' said Martha.

'Test me then,' said Opal, 'if you don't believe me.'

'All right, I will. What colour underpants is Robbie wearing today?'

'Ah well, that's a trick question,' said Opal. 'Because he's wearing two pairs. He's got Spider-Man ones on over some red ones.'

'Hey! Do you mind?' said Robbie, hitching up his jeans although they were not hanging down. 'Some things on Earth are private, you know.'

'Sorry,' said Opal, 'but your sister did ask.'

Martha shrugged. 'Lucky guess,' she said in an effort to cover her astonishment. 'Anyway, Robbie, you really should let Mum wash those Spider-Man pants sometimes.'

'No way,' said Robbie. 'They're my favourites.'

They were safely past the salon by now but Martha couldn't help glancing round, half-expecting to see Mum rushing after them to ask where on earth they were going. There was just one man trailing along the pavement behind them. It was the same man who had been standing by the milk float eating scotch eggs, the one Martha thought must be the milkman. He didn't look so dazed now. He looked gloomy instead, bumbling along with his hands shoved deep in his pockets, and muttering to himself.

Opal on the other hand was in very high spirits. She kept hopping and leaping about, dodging the cracks in the paving stones. Looking at her, Martha guessed she must be about her own age, nine or ten or so, and yet here she was bobbing around like a four-year-old.

'We don't have cracks in the pavement in Carnelia,' said Opal, as if in explanation. 'In fact we don't have pavements.' She took an enormous jump over a huge paving slab. 'And we certainly don't have any cracks.'

'But if you don't have pavements,' panted Robbie, trying to follow Opal's zigzag route, 'what do you actually walk on?'

'Oh, we don't walk much at all,' said Opal. 'Generally, we glide.'

'Wow!' said Robbie. 'Is that because there's not much gravity on Carnelia?'

'That's it,' answered Opal. 'If you want to get moving, you just jump up and start swimming. Obviously if we're in a major hurry we take the Shmockledrain.' She hop-scotched away.

'Shmockledrain!' Robbie stood still in awe.

Martha looked at him. 'Robbie, you know they've taken the word "gullible" out of the dictionary, don't you?'

Robbie's eyes widened still further. '*Have* they?'

Then he realised and gave Martha a shove. 'Very funny! Zack's done that joke on me before. Come on, she's getting away from us.'

Opal twirled and skipped along at great speed so that Martha and Robbie had to run to catch up. They reached the mini-market in no time. Opal bounced onto the floor pad that triggered the automatic door, gave a whoop of delight, swooped inside and bounded straight into a shopping trolley.

'Wayhey!' she cried. 'You've got sledspangles after all. Things are looking up!'

She stood in the trolley with her eyes closed for a moment, then opened them, clearly disappointed. 'We haven't gone very far, have we? Maybe this one's not working.' She ran her hands along the trolley's metal caging. 'Or does it have an "on" button? Come on, you two, how are you supposed to drive this thing?'

Martha didn't know whether to walk away and pretend Opal had nothing to do with her, or to laugh out loud. Instead she whispered to her to get out of the trolley.

'*You* don't go in it, idiot! Your shopping does!'

'Shame,' replied Opal. 'I was looking forward to a quick whizz round the clock.' She stood up and balanced as if she was on a skateboard, making the trolley jerk from side to side.

'Will you get out of there!' Martha hissed. Robbie was no use. He was giggling uncontrollably and looking likely to fall backwards into a shelf-load of red apples.

'All right, keep your hat on. I'm coming. Give me your hands, will you?' They took a hand each and Opal, with a loud '*yeeha*', jumped out of the trolley. It was a high, kicking kind of jump and she only

narrowly avoided hitting a passing shopper with one of her big silver boots.

'So sorry, my lady.' Opal bowed low. 'I really should look where I'm loping.' The woman frowned and continued on her way. 'Have an exciting day!' Opal bellowed after her. 'I know I'm going to.'

Any more of this and they would be thrown out. Martha could already see the store's security guard staring at them and fiddling with his walkie talkie. Quickly she steered Opal, Robbie and the trolley away up the fruit and vegetable aisle. But it wasn't long before Opal was running ahead and picking things up gleefully. She selected four oranges, snapped off a banana and began juggling them all.

'What do you do with these crazy things?' she said. She threw the fruits one at a time to Martha who did her best to catch them and put them in the trolley.

'Eat them, of course,' she said. She tried to look serious. After all, someone had to be sensible, but it was difficult when you were holding a banana in one hand, an orange in the crook of your elbow and another one under your chin.

'Don't you have fruit on Carnelia?' asked Robbie.

'Not likely,' said Opal. 'We get all our nourishment from scoff capsules. They're only as big as these things.' She poked a bag of small green grapes with her finger. 'And you only need three of them to feel completely full. We don't need any of this huge stuff you've got here.'

'What do scoff capsules taste of?' said Robbie.

'Taste of?' Opal seemed puzzled. 'Nothing. They

don't have a taste. They're just capsules.'

'Do you mean you've never tasted real food?' said Martha.

Opal shook her head. 'Nope.'

'You mean you've never had crisps, or Space Nuggets, or chocolate, or ice cream?' Robbie couldn't believe it. 'That is the saddest thing I've heard in my entire life!'

Martha held up a carrot. 'Do you even know what one of these tastes like?'

'Haven't got the fizziest idea,' said Opal. 'What is it?'

'A carrot.'

'Ah, a carrot.' Opal nodded wisely. Then she bit the top off the carrot, threw back her head and attempted to swallow it. At once she began to choke and Martha had to bang her on the back until the piece of carrot dislodged itself and shot out across the floor.

'You're supposed to chew it first,' said Martha. She was beginning to think Opal might be telling the truth about being an alien after all. Anyone who had lived on Earth for more than a few years would know it was stupid to try to eat a carrot without using their teeth.

'Silly old me!' said Opal, coughing. She looked up. 'Oops a rosie, I seem to have attracted a little fan club.'

It was true. The three of them were now almost entirely hemmed in by shopping trolleys as other customers stopped to watch Opal's antics. For someone so keen not to draw attention to herself, Opal was managing to stand out like a very sore, very purple thumb.

'What's the matter with you lot?' she said merrily. 'Never seen anyone jet-vomiting carrots before?' She put her hands on her hips and stuck out her remarkably long tongue, causing the shoppers to flinch in surprise.

'Opal, tell you what,' said Martha as calmly as she could manage. 'Let's just do the shopping and go, shall we?'

She led the way quickly through the group of onlookers. Robbie pushed the trolley and Opal came behind with lots of 'excuse me's and 'pardon us's and elaborate bowing and curtseying.

'Will you please just try to act normally for half a minute!' begged Martha.

'Of course, Martha,' said Opal in some surprise. 'Your wish is my demand.'

'Command!' said Martha. Opal really was annoying. Still, she did need to eat. Martha had to admit that. She began to shop in earnest. She picked things off the shelves and tossed them into the trolley. Robbie did too. While he brought cereal, biscuits, jelly, and several packets of his favourite sweets, Martha chose sliced bread, muffins, jam, tins of soup, butter, milk and yoghurt. She was really getting into her stride. She selected dried apricots and raisins, nuts and crackers, fruit juice and cheese. She thought of the empty flat where Opal was living. She would need other things too, not just food. Toilet paper and toothpaste, soap and a hairbrush; she didn't look as if she owned a hairbrush.

Opal followed Martha and Robbie around,

humming to herself. She kept her hands pushed firmly into her pockets and she didn't grab anything off the shelves. Martha could see she really was trying to behave like a regular human being and blend in. Somehow, though, it didn't work. People still turned to stare at her as they passed. The sunglasses didn't help. What normal person did their supermarket shopping in shades? But then, if she took them off people would see her eyes and *they* were stranger than strange.

'I'll need something for them, you know,' said Opal.

'For what?'

'For my eyes.'

Martha realised she had been tuning into her thoughts again. 'I've told you not to do that,' she said indignantly. 'It's a very irritating habit.'

'Sorry,' said Opal. 'My eyes are terribly nosey, aren't they? I know, I'll send them a memo, tell them to quit it.' She stood stock still and went cross-eyed for a moment and then let her eyes bounce back to normal. 'That should do it,' she said cheerily. 'Anyway, what *have* they got for eyes?'

'There's eyewash,' said Martha. She thought for a moment. 'And cucumbers. Cucumber slices are meant to be very soothing for eyes.'

Robbie was sent off in search of cucumbers while Opal helped herself to eighteen boxes of eyewash. It was all that was on the shelf. 'What?' she said, seeing Martha's disapproving expression. 'A Moonbaby has to look after her eyes, you know. A Moonbaby's eyes are a Moonbaby's fortune.'

Martha sighed and looked at the brimming trolley.

She wondered how much money Opal had with her. She was just about to ask her when Garnet stuck his head out of Opal's pocket and made a noise that was neither a miaow, nor a bark, nor a squeak. Whatever it was, it was a complaining sound and it was very insistent.

'Darn it, Garnet! Don't make such a fuss. We haven't forgotten about you. What shall we do, Martha? Garnet's got the crunchies.'

'Munchies,' said Martha, scanning the shelves for pet food. What would a mingle like to eat? They paused by guinea pig food, then dog food, then fish food. When they reached the cat food Garnet scrabbled out of Opal's pocket and climbed up onto her head. He sat there kneading her hat with his feline claws and drooling.

Opal picked out a box of dry cat food, tore off the cardboard top and tossed a few rings of food up to Garnet. He caught them in his mouth and cracked them up hungrily.

'Um, I don't think you should do that,' began Martha, but Opal tossed up more and more handfuls as they continued down the aisle. Garnet couldn't catch them all at once and soon the girls were crunching dry cat food underfoot.

'You're supposed to pay for it first,' said Martha. She began to lead the way quickly towards the check-out.

'Got you!' said a loud voice behind her. Martha felt her heart lurch. 'Got you, you little troublemaker! I knew it was you. I knew it the minute I saw you!'

Martha turned, expecting to see the security guard come to tell them off for abusing shopping trolleys, spitting carrots and scattering cat food. But it wasn't the security guard. It was the gloomy milkman she had seen in the street. He didn't look so gloomy now. He looked angry. He was holding onto Opal's shoulders and shaking her.

'You made me crash, you did. You and that flying animal of yours. Got me the sack, you did. Made me the laughing stock of the depot, you have. No one believes me but I know what I saw. Take those glasses off so I can see your eyes. Go on, you take them off!'

He made a lunge for Opal's sunglasses. She ducked and his hands met Garnet who was still sitting on her head.

'Where's his wings then? Where's his wings?' He began patting Garnet's body all over, searching for wings. Garnet hissed and growled and bared his tiny diamond teeth.

Martha was shocked at the way the man had grabbed hold of Opal and the nasty way he was handling Garnet. She hated it when people were rough like that; it always made her feel like crying. 'Let him go!' she said. 'Leave them alone. They haven't done you any harm.'

'That's all you know,' said the man, still frisking Garnet vigorously, making him yelp.

Opal bobbed up and adjusted her hat, which had become squashed down over her glasses. 'Unhand my beast at once,' she said in a very royal sort of voice.

'It is essential that you release him this billisecond!'

The man ignored her and went on pressing and pummelling Garnet, pulling his fur in all directions.

Just then Robbie came round the corner, carrying an enormous cucumber. Robbie had already become very fond of Garnet. Even though the mingle made him sneeze he still loved stroking him and watching his funny mixed-up animal behaviour. Seeing this man grappling with the cutest creature he had ever met, Robbie didn't think twice. He swung the cucumber like a rounders bat and walloped the man in the back of the knees. The man yowled in pain and stumbled to the floor.

'Oh, great,' he moaned. 'First you lose me my job and now you're setting your human minions on me, getting them to break my legs. Talk about insult to injury!'

Opal took the opportunity to whisk Garnet out of the man's hands and tuck him out of sight in her cape pocket. 'My good male,' she said. 'I'm quite sure I don't know what you're bunnying on about. I've never seen you before in my Earthly life.'

'Well, I've seen you,' said the man. He made as if to get up but changed his mind when he saw Robbie, still standing over him with the now rather bendy cucumber. 'I've seen you in the dead of night. You've got weird eyes behind them glasses. Lit up like a pair of lighthouses, they did. Completely dazzled, I was. Where are you from? You tell me that! I ought to report you. I ought to go to the police!'

'Hello there, young ladies and gentleman. Is this

fellow troubling you?' Now it really was the security guard. He was strolling towards them, taking his time. 'Shall I sort him out for you?'

'It's not me that needs sorting out,' insisted the man. 'It's her.' He jabbed a finger at Opal. 'She's the one that's trouble. Her and her flying fox. I've lost my job because of them. You ought to arrest her for causing an accident. She should own up to what she is, she should.'

'And what's that, sir?' said the security guard.

'An alien!' said the man in a loud voice. 'She's an alien! She's from another planet!'

Martha held her breath. Were they about to be arrested? Would they all be marched off to the police station? What would Mum say?

'An alien is she, sir?' said the security guard, stroking his beard. He winked at Martha. 'Yes, yes, of course she is.' He patted the man on the back and began to help him to his feet. 'This little girl's an alien, we're in Buckingham Palace and I'm Cinderella coming to the party. How do you like my ball gown?' He picked up his imaginary skirts and did a little dance. 'Now why don't you come along with me and we'll let these good people go about their business?'

He led the man firmly away. Martha could hear him saying, 'She's an alien, an alien I tell you, an alien, I know what I saw, an alien ...' His voice trailed off as he disappeared round the corner.

Martha, Robbie and Opal looked at one another, daring to breathe again.

'Right,' said Martha. 'Time we checked out.'

C hecking out should have been simple enough, but Opal made it almost impossible. She was thrilled by the mini-market's brand new conveyor belt and kept putting her hands flat on it and gliding up to the check-out. Each time she reached the end she said, '*Yeeha!*' and started again. Martha and Robbie had to work round her, feeding the shopping through the gaps under her armpits.

To make matters even more difficult, Opal decided that it would be fun for Garnet to have a ride. She popped him onto the conveyor belt and he sat calmly washing his fur as he sailed towards the check-out. The man at the check-out didn't notice him at first. He was absent-mindedly picking up each item of shopping as it came to hand, scanning it and putting it into the shopping bags.

But then Garnet reached the end of the check-out

and the man picked him up by the neck and tried to swipe him, just like any other bit of shopping. Garnet was most put out and grabbed the man's hand with all four paws, digging in his claws. He growled a fierce little growl. '*Chi-chi-chi-chigga!*'

'*Ra-ra-ra-rat!*' whispered the man hoarsely, holding the indignant mingle just millimetres from his face. In his shock he couldn't make any real sound come out at first. Then he found his voice and let out a huge ear-piercing scream. 'Ahhhhhhh! Rat! Help! Giant rat! Raaaattttt! Help me!' he shrieked, quickly dropping Garnet, who slid down the slope towards the carrier bags and then sat up on his hind legs, scolding the man with a stream of irate chattering. He hated being called a rat.

'That's not a rat,' said a woman who was stacking a nearby shelf with tins of soup. 'That's a mongoose.'

'A meerkat, you mean,' said a customer waiting in line.

'Call the RSPCA!' shouted someone.

'Call the zoo!' yelled someone else. 'It's a wild cat. It's a baby ocelot!'

'Catch it! Catch it, whatever it is!' cried the checkout man, clutching his hand. 'Ooh, I think it bit me. I'm going to get rabies. Horrible dirty thing!'

Opal picked Garnet up. 'My dear male,' she began. 'This animal is not dirty. He is as clean as your whistle and as white as your feather. And he does not bite. Although if you'd just yelled in *my* ear like that, I think I would have been tempted to give you a little nip myself.'

Martha was watching shoppers emerge from the various aisles, curious to see what was going on. She saw the security guard ambling towards them again. She grabbed Opal's sleeve. 'Opal,' she said urgently. 'We've got to get out of here. Now!'

'Ah,' said Opal, looking round. 'See what you mean.' She turned back to the flabbergasted check-out man. 'I'd love to stay and chat but I'm afraid I have to evacuate. Cheery-bye.'

With that she crammed Garnet into her pocket, leaped over the trolley and raced through the exit, her purple cape flying behind her. Martha and Robbie had to push their way around the trolley before they could follow her, but just as they reached the doors, the security guard appeared in their path.

'Fancy meeting you again so soon,' he said. 'Lovely lot of shopping you've got there.' He gestured towards the abandoned trolley which was brimming with bags of the groceries they had collected. 'Got the money to pay for all that, have you?'

Martha felt in her pocket and found a five pence piece. She knew the shopping must add up to a hundred pounds or more. She shook her head, her face reddening with embarrassment.

'No,' said the guard. 'Didn't think so. But you weren't going to leave it all there, were you? For someone else to put back?'

Martha kept her eyes fixed on the floor. 'No,' she mumbled.

'Because that would be a bit thoughtless, wouldn't

it? And I can tell you aren't the thoughtless type, are you now?'

Martha shook her head.

'And you aren't thoughtless either, are you, young man?' The guard drew Robbie out from behind Martha's back where he had been trying to keep a low profile.

'No,' Robbie said meekly.

'So the pair of you can get busy and put all that away, and we'll overlook it, just this once, all right?'

'OK,' muttered Robbie.

'Thank you,' whispered Martha.

'Right you are, everyone,' said the security guard to the audience of shoppers. 'The show's over. But come back tomorrow for the next exciting instalment of the mini-market matinée. Aliens, robbers, wild animals, we've got it all here, it's better than the circus!' He bowed low, chuckling to himself, and the gaggle of shoppers began to disperse.

☆ ✴ ✻

Putting everything back on the shelves took much longer than dumping it in the trolley had done. Martha worked quickly. She was sure Mum would be looking for them by now. She would be really worried if she couldn't find them. She and Robbie ran back and forth among the fruit and vegetables, returning apples and oranges and tomatoes to their rightful places. They spent ages in Biscuits and Confectionery because Robbie had gone a bit mad

70

collecting chocolate, sweets and cookies. He ran ahead tossing it all willy nilly onto the shelves, while Martha came behind trying to make it look tidy again.

She wished she'd never agreed to bring Opal to the mini-market. It had been a terrible idea. What should have been a simple shopping expedition to buy a few bits and pieces had turned into a complete and total disaster. Opal Moonbaby had caused a whole load of trouble and now she had flitted off somewhere, leaving her and Robbie behind to sort it all out. This was turning into the most embarrassing day ever. Martha was just thinking that it couldn't get any worse, when it did.

Chloe and Colette were standing at the top of the aisle, watching and sniggering behind their hands. They hadn't been heading for the swings after all. They had been heading for the mini-market. Just her luck. Martha did her best to ignore them but when she needed to push the trolley round to the next aisle they were right in her way.

'Oh, hello, Martha,' said Colette, pretending she had only just seen her there. 'Doing a bit of shopping, are you?'

'Something like that,' Martha answered, trying unsuccessfully to manoeuvre the trolley between them.

'Only the thing is,' Colette grinned knowingly at Chloe, 'I don't think you've quite got the hang of it. You're supposed to put the shopping *in* the trolley, not take it out. Didn't you know?'

71

'Excuse me, please,' said Martha. 'You're in my way.'

'Are we? Oh, sorry! I didn't realise,' said Colette in mock surprise. She knew perfectly well she was blocking Martha's path. She was doing it on purpose.

'What's the problem?' said Chloe. 'Did you forget to bring enough cash with you?'

'Yeah,' said Colette. 'Did you forget to bring your pocket money?' She leaned over the trolley. 'What is all this stuff anyway?' She picked up the open packet of dried cat biscuits. 'Oh look, Chloe! She's been snacking on cat food. Ugh, that is gross!' She gazed at Martha with wide eyes. 'Martha, have you been playing at being a little kitty cat?'

The two of them collapsed in a fit of giggles which allowed Martha enough time to push past them, her cheeks burning with fury and embarrassment.

'*So babyish!*' snorted Colette as she passed. They began to snigger again. They called after her, 'Here, pussy! Here, kitty kitty!' and their laughter followed her through the mini-market and out of the doors.

8

Chloe and Colette's laughter rang in Martha's ears for the rest of the day. She could hear it as she and Robbie ran back to the salon. She could hear it as Mum told them off for straying too far from the play area. She could hear it as she munched her way laboriously through her sandwiches. She could still hear it when they went back outside to find Opal stretched out in the sun, her silver boots on the grass beside her, waggling her extremely long toes in the air.

'Thanks for a fantabulous morning, Earth dwellers!' she said. 'That was the best fun I've had since I landed!'

'Fun?' Martha cried. 'Fun? We just caused total mayhem in the supermarket. We almost got attacked by an angry mob. We practically got arrested. And you call that fun?' She shook her head at Opal.

'We didn't even manage to get the shopping for you.'

'Well at least I remembered these,' answered Opal, holding up a carrier bag full of eyewash and the bent cucumber that Robbie had used to bring down the man in the mini-market. She broke it in half and applied the moist insides to her eyes. 'Ah, lovely,' she breathed.

Martha clapped a hand to her forehead in disbelief. 'Oh, great! So now we're thieves as well. You haven't paid for that, you know!'

Opal removed the cucumber halves for a moment. 'Paid?' she said. She looked confused, as if she had never heard the word. She flickered her eyes. She was accessing her dictionary again. '*Paid*,' she read. '*Verb. To pay. Give someone money for something so that you can have it*. Oh, now I understand.' She paused and scratched her head. 'What's money?'

Martha sighed. 'Look, on Earth, you have to . . . I mean you can't just take stuff you want. You need money to pay for it, pound coins, 50ps and ten-pound notes and things.'

'Let's get some of those, then,' said Opal.

'It's not that easy. Unless you have a bank account or a credit card. Do you have one of those?'

In reply, Opal's stomach let out an enormous grumble. Of course Opal didn't have a credit card. She didn't even know what money was. As far as Martha could tell she was completely unprepared for life as a human being. If she really was an alien, whoever had organised her trip to Earth had clearly not done their research properly. Opal was going to need a lot of help just to survive.

Martha sighed. 'We'll get you some food, OK? But tomorrow. We can't do anything before then. You'll have to wait until tomorrow.'

Opal leaped up and gave Martha a massive bone-crunching hug. 'Oh, thank you! Thank you! You're a real friend. You're my best friend. I love you. Do you love me? You do, don't you? Say you do!'

Martha struggled to free herself from Opal's iron grip. If she squeezed any harder she was going to break her ribs. She wrenched herself away.

'Of course I don't love you! And I'm not your friend. I just feel sorry for you, that's all. I'd do the same for anyone.'

'Oh!' Opal's arms dropped to her sides. She looked like a dog that had been sent to lie in the corner in disgrace.

'I'm your friend,' offered Robbie.

'Thanks, cucumber hero,' said Opal, but she still looked downcast.

'And anyway, Opal,' said Martha. 'What about that man?'

'What man?'

'The man in the supermarket. The man who said you made him crash his float.'

'Oh, him,' said Opal airily. 'I don't know anything about him. He was raving bonkers. Mad as a box of hogs. I mean, a box of snogs, or is it dogs?'

'It's frogs!' said Robbie, laughing.

'Right,' said Opal. 'Mad as a box of frogs. Great

big spotty ones.' She began to hop about, croaking. 'Never seen the man before in my life. *Croak*. He's quite clearly off his rocket. *Croak croak*. Anyway, you know what they say,' she crowed. 'There's no use sighing over spilled milk!'

Martha watched as Opal and Robbie hopped around together, making ribbiting noises. She glanced at Garnet who was curled up on the bottom of the slide, his whiskers glinting in the sunshine. He did look a bit like a flying fox, just as the man had said. It *must* have been them in the road that night. It couldn't have been anyone else. She narrowed her eyes as a thought came to her. 'How did you know it was milk?' she said.

'What?' said Opal. She stopped hopping for a moment.

'You said it was spilled milk. No one else mentioned milk. That man is the milkman and there was a lot of spilled milk. All over the road. You must have seen it. You *were* there, weren't you? It *was* your fault he crashed, wasn't it?'

Opal flopped down on the grass. 'Not entirely,' she said. 'It wasn't my fault he was eating a giant pastry puffball and his mind was on cake. He should have been more careful.' She began hopping around and croaking again, as if that was the end of the matter.

Martha felt anger bubbling up inside her. 'Thanks to you,' she said, 'I have just had the most horrific morning ever. Thanks to you, Robbie and I have just got into massive trouble with our mum. Thanks to you, that man has lost his job and all you can do is make fun of him. You should be ashamed of yourself, Opal Moonbaby! What kind of an alien are you?'

Opal stopped croaking and sat back on her haunches. 'So you *do* believe I'm an alien, then?'

Martha shrugged. She felt trapped. 'Maybe you are and maybe you aren't. I don't know. But I know one thing – you don't have a single proper human feeling. Don't you feel guilty or sorry? Don't you feel a bit sorry for what you've done to that milkman? You should be thinking about how to help him, not dancing around like some idiotic purple toad!'

There was a brief silence. It was broken by a strange sound. The muffled, musical sound of a large bell ringing deep under water.

'S'cuse me a milli-minute,' said Opal. 'I'd better get that. It's the hydrophone. Uncle Bixbite will be calling to find how out how I'm getting on.' She rushed over to the fence that enclosed the paddling pool and vaulted over it.

'Hydrophone?' said Robbie.

'Uncle *Bixbite*?' said Martha.

This they had to see.

☆ ☆ ☆

They scrambled over the fence and hid behind a bush. They didn't really know why they were hiding. It just seemed like the right thing to do. Opal was standing by the pool, her arms outstretched. Her sunglasses were on the top of her head now and her eyes were closed. Garnet sat at her feet, gazing expectantly into the water.

'Maybe the Loch Ness monster's in there,' Robbie whispered. It was meant to be a joke but just then the water in the pool began to undulate, pushing little waves out to the sides. The sky seemed to darken and the pool gave off a hazy blue steam. The water glowed and, as they watched, a dark shape rippled into view. It was large and long. Garnet sat up and started to bark-squeak, wagging his stubby tail vigorously. Robbie whispered, '*Nessie!*' and he and Martha linked arms.

As the shape grew stronger and clearer they saw that it wasn't a monster, but a man. A man, fully dressed in a royal blue suit and wearing a black bow tie, was lying in the paddling pool, under the water. It wasn't the whole of him. It was just the front. He looked as though he had been ironed like a sheet and he was so light that he was wafting about in the water. He seemed very peaceful, his hands folded across his middle and water lapping gently around his diamond-shaped ears.

He opened his eyes. They were blue. They were the brightest, bluest eyes you have ever seen. Much brighter than any human's eyes, or any animal's eyes come to that. And as he opened his eyes, beams of blue light shot out of them, illuminating Opal who was still standing at the water's edge. She opened her own eyes and looked directly at the man. Immediately her eyes sent dazzling violet rays back to him. The meeting of their light beams was so bright and the colours so vivid that Martha and Robbie, still clutching one another, had to shield their eyes with their hands.

From under the water, the man spoke. If you could call it speaking.

'Dalrebeyseydazzzzxxxxi,' is what he said.

'Xxxxyadibrovnexxx,' Opal replied. Then she said, 'Do speak in English, Uncle Bixie, won't you? I have made an oath, don't forget.' She clutched her ear lobes, stood on one leg and, assuming a very solemn expression, said,

'I do promise to only utter
English words like bed and butter,
Backwards, forwards, head and gutter.
No Carnelian shall pass my lips
Only sandwiches and felt tips.'

'Very well,' her uncle's voice bubbled back. 'Good for you, Opal. Glad to see you're taking a challenge seriously for once. How are you adapting to human life?'

'Oh, I'm taking to it like a truck to water,' said Opal, letting go of her ears and dropping her raised leg.

'And the arrival? Smooth and silent, I trust?'

'Extremely.'

'And quite unnoticed? No one spotted the space capsule?'

'Completely unnoticed!' said Opal emphatically. That wasn't true, thought Martha. The milkman had noticed her arrival all right.

'So no problems with the newspapers then. No journalists. No photographers following you around.'

'Zero photographers,' said Opal, making zero signs with both hands.

'Because you know if some non-certified human takes your photo and reveals your true identity, that means instant failure. The consequences for you will be both serious and severe.'

'Oh consequences, shmonsequences!' Opal shrugged. 'No need to worry about them. I'm blending in perfectly. I've been following the Earth Manual to the letter. The Moonbabies will win the Carnelian Coronet again this light-year, no problem. It'll be like taking brandy from a baby.'

'Good,' said Uncle Bixbite, apparently reassured. 'Well, that sounds like the first two parts of your challenge are proceeding well. What about Part Three?'

'Oh fine.' Opal waved her hands as if she wanted to wave away the subject of 'Part Three'.

'So you've located the target?'

'Yes, that's right, absolutely,' said Opal quickly in a rather too loud voice. 'It's all under control. My CIA is practically in the box. Leave it to me, Uncle Bixie. Anyway I'd better be off, got a lot of being human to get on with, you know. See you on Ascendance Night.'

Then she held up one hand and crossed it with the palm of the other. 'Vatengpaxxz,' she said.

'Vatengpaxxz, Opal,' said Uncle Bixbite, making

the same sign. And with one last watery ripple he was gone. The lights faded, the blue steam subsided and the sun came out from behind a cloud. Robbie rushed over to the edge of the paddling pool where the water was fizzing like lemonade. He put in his hand, then pulled it back instantly.

'Ow, that's boiling! If I fell in there, I'd be a total casualty!'

'What d'you expect?' said Opal breezily. 'A hydrophone is a very high-energy appliance. Uncle Bixbite was on the line all the way from Carnelia, you know. That's a zillion light-decades further away from Earth than the furthest star in your entire solar system. Of course the hydrophone needs plenty of heat. How's it going to work otherwise?'

Robbie sucked his scalded fingers. 'Well, Martha, even you must believe in Carnelia now. You do believe Opal's an actual alien, don't you? Come on, yes or no?'

Martha didn't want to believe it. It was crazy to believe it. But there was no longer any room for doubt. She took a deep breath. 'Yes,' she said.

'Whoopee!' crowed Opal. 'Then we're halfway there!'

'Halfway where?' asked Robbie.

'Oh, nowhere,' said Opal, staring up at the sky.

'What's the Carnelian Coronet?' said Martha.

'It's what all Carnelian clans want,' said Opal. 'If you hold the Coronet you get to make the rules. The Moonbabies are the best rule-makers of all. "Fair and Share", that's the Moonbaby motto. Everyone's happy when we're in charge. Uncle Bixbite's held the Coronet for the last eighteen light-years. Everybody loves him, life on Carnelia is sweet and we need to keep it that way. You don't want the Coronet falling into the wrong hands. Imagine if the Mercurials got hold of it. They'd turn Carnelia downside up in an instant.'

'Could they get hold of it?' said Robbie.

'Not very likely,' answered Opal. 'But the thing is there are lots of them. The Mercurials are a very big clan now and they need watching. If they collect gazillions of planet points they could start causing big trouble. That's why Moonbaby cadets like me have to make sure we get our Carnelian Independence Awards, so we can add to the Moonbaby planet pot.'

'I see,' said Martha, still puzzling over all this new information. 'But I was wondering, Opal, what's Part Three of your Carnelian Independence Award all about? There *is* a Part Three, isn't there? And what's the target?'

Opal didn't seem to have heard. 'Oh look, Earthlings,' she said. 'Your mum's just about to come outside. You'd better skedaddle. Don't forget to come tomorrow though. Garnet and I are going to fade away into the atmosphere if we don't eat soon.'

'OK,' said Martha. 'But wait a minute, will you? There's something else I want to know.'

'Quick quick! She's on her way,' said Opal. 'Come on, I'll give you a leg on.'

'Leg *up*,' corrected Robbie, as Opal cupped her long hands together, offering him a foothold to climb back over the fence.

'See you tomorrow,' she said. 'Be bright and squirly and don't forget the edibles!'

Martha had a great many questions to ask. What was Ascendance Night? What was this mysterious 'Part Three' of the challenge? What was the target Uncle Bixbite had been talking about, and why did Opal always change the subject whenever it was mentioned? But Martha knew now that Opal really could see as far as she claimed. She didn't want to get into trouble with Mum again so she too scrambled over the fence and back to the salon. The questions would have to wait.

'Mum?' Martha said as they ate their tea that evening.

'Mmmm?' Mum was studying a magazine of the latest hairstyles. Alesha had been moaning that although Mum was very good at haircutting, the styles she knew were all out of date. According to Alesha, Mum was 'well behind the times', so Mum was doing all she could to catch up with them.

'If you knew someone who didn't have any food or money or anything, what would you do?'

'Try and help them I suppose,' answered Mum, still absorbed in the magazine and making notes on a pad beside her.

'I mean, even if they were a bit odd, a bit peculiar? Even if they didn't always stick to the rules?'

Mum tapped her chin with her pen, considering.

Martha waited. She couldn't tell if Mum was thinking about the book or her question. At last Mum said, 'Yes, I think I probably would help them, if I could. As long as I wasn't doing anything really wrong myself. Yes, I'm sure I would.'

So that's it, thought Martha. She knew now what she would do. She would help Opal Moonbaby. She would help her find food and live comfortably on Earth. She would try to stop anyone finding out that she was an alien or taking photos of her. She didn't know what the 'serious and severe' consequences of that happening could be, but whatever they were, they sounded pretty nasty. She wondered why Opal had told her and Robbie that she was an alien. She didn't seem to mind *them* knowing. Why wasn't she worried that they would reveal her secret? Maybe it was because she liked showing off so much, she couldn't resist telling someone. Whatever the reason, Martha didn't like the idea of anything really horrible happening to Opal so she would try to protect her and show her the ways of the world. Because when you thought about it, Earth would be a pretty strange place to visit if you didn't know what was what.

She would do all this for Opal but she would not be her friend. This wasn't friendship. This was just helping someone in need. There was a big difference. After all, Martha was never going to make friends with anyone ever again. She hadn't changed her mind about that. Her thoughts wandered for a moment into that painful part of her memory, into what had happened with the Secret Circle. She thought of

Chloe and Colette laughing at her in the mini-market. She shuddered.

'Are you feeling all right, Martha?'

Martha looked up and realised that Mum had stopped studying her hairstyles magazine and was studying her instead. 'Yes,' she said. 'I'm fine.'

'Only you would tell me, wouldn't you, if there was anything wrong? Anything worrying you?'

'Of course.' Martha smiled. She couldn't possibly tell Mum anything about Opal Moonbaby. And anyway, there wasn't one bit of the story she would believe.

Robbie came in with a plate of toast piled high with baked beans, Yoyo sitting on top of the pile. 'Beans, beans, good for the heart,' he chanted. 'The more you eat, the more you—'

'Ah, Robbie,' Mum interrupted. 'Zack's mum phoned. They're back from Cornwall. She said you could go over there to play tomorrow if you like.'

Robbie licked tomato sauce off Yoyo's legs. 'Nah, no thanks. I'd rather go to the salon actually.'

Mum's jaw dropped. 'What? But Zack's your best friend! You hate the salon!'

'It's OK there now,' said Robbie. 'And I don't want to miss seeing . . . I mean, I don't want to leave Martha all on her own. It wouldn't be fair.'

Mum shook her head but she was clearly pleased. 'Well,' she said, 'how gallant is that! You want to look after your big sister. Isn't that thoughtful, Martha?'

'Very,' said Martha. Though she knew Robbie's reasons for wanting to stay close to the salon had nothing whatsoever to do with her.

✳ ✳ ✳

The next day she and Robbie arrived at A Cut Above armed with carrier bags and a plan. They told Mum the bags were filled with the toys and games they were planning to play with during the day.

As expected, Alesha shooed them straight into the storeroom. They made a beeline for the little window and stood with their eyes fixed on the entrance to the ground floor flats, waiting for Opal to appear. Quite soon she came bursting out of the door, sticking Garnet on her head and flinging her cape around her shoulders. In a few loping strides she reached the concrete play pipe, jumped on top of it and stood there waving her arms like enthusiastic windmills.

'Now!' said Martha. And she held up a bent pen lid.

Robbie took a breath. 'That's mine!' he said in a loud voice.

'No it isn't,' Martha said in an equally loud voice. 'It's mine!'

'Give it back!' shouted Robbie.

'No way! I found it. It belongs to me!'

'Does not!'

'Does too!'

'You're a selfish stinky pig!' Robbie grinned.

'Well, you're a mean, greedy little monster!'

Martha picked up a giant tub of shampoo and slammed it down on the floor. 'Ow!' she cried.

Robbie picked up a box of brand new towels and slammed that down too. 'Gerroff me!' he yelled. 'You great big ugly bully!'

'Bum head!'

'Snot face!'

'Poo brain!'

That was all that was needed. Alesha charged in like a highly miffed rhinoceros.

'Outside!' she shouted. 'No fighting in my salon and no language of the toiletto!' She followed them through the salon ranting about crazy no-hoper kids. Mum, who was in the middle of wrapping strips of tin foil round a client's hair, shook her head sadly as they passed.

'I'm ashamed of you both,' she said.

They clutched their carrier bags and tried to look contrite. That part wasn't difficult for Martha. She hated being a disappointment to Mum but she couldn't let Opal starve.

✦ ✦ ✦

'My first Earth sandwich!' exclaimed Opal, taking it out of one of the carrier bags. She rubbed it gently against her cheek, kissed it, then folded it into her mouth and swallowed it whole. There was a short pause and then Opal let out a long and very loud burp. 'I did an Earth belch!' she said joyfully. 'I've always wanted to do one of those. Now what does the Earth Manual say you have to do?' She cleared her throat. 'Pardon me, dude, for being so rude. It was not my food, but me that mooed!'

'Did you like it?' said Robbie. 'Was it as good as a scoff capsule?'

Opal looked thoughtful. 'It was spongier,' she said. 'And softer. And breadier. And butterier. And yes, all right, maybe even a tiny bit better. Just a pigeon.'

'Smidgeon!' said Martha.

'Just a smidgeon,' agreed Opal.

'Hooray!' cried Robbie. 'Earth – one, Carnelia – nil!' He chalked up the scores in the air. 'It's the first time that's happened.'

'And the last,' said Opal contentedly, as she unloaded the rest of the things. Martha had brought the bread and butter. She had also smuggled a carton of milk from the fridge, as well as her old baby blanket and a cushion she thought would make Opal more comfortable in the empty flat.

Robbie's bag contained three sweets, his fourth-best toy car, a pack of wild animal top trumps, and a large cake tin padded out with cotton wool for Garnet to sleep in.

Opal lined the things up on the concrete pipe to admire them. Garnet jumped off her head and into the cake tin. He looked at Robbie and said *cheeweechee*. Then he turned round three times, curled up in a ball and went to sleep. Opal clapped her hands together with glee.

'What glorious gifts!' she declared. She picked up the carton of milk and held it reverently in both hands. 'Martha,' she said. 'This box of dairy goods is a symbol of your first act of friendship towards me. I shall never drink it. Not a drop. I will keep it and treasure it for ever.'

Martha laughed. 'It's not an act of friendship, Opal. It's a pint of milk. And I wouldn't keep it if I were you. Milk turns into yukky smelly cheese if you don't drink it in a day or two.'

'Oh!' said Opal. 'Right you are then.' And she opened the carton and poured it down her throat. She didn't even pause to swallow. The milk just glugged down inside her like water down the bathroom plughole. She drained the last drop and wiped her mouth with the back of her hand. 'Mm,' she said. 'Very cow-tasting. Very cow-tasting indeed. Now, where are you taking me?'

'Taking you?' said Martha. 'We're not taking you anywhere. Remember what happened last time we let you persuade us to go somewhere? No, we're staying right here.'

'Oh, go on!' said Opal. 'I want to see the sights of Earth. There can't be many of them so it won't take the two of you long to give me a quick tour.'

'Not many sights?' protested Martha. 'You *are* joking! What about the pyramids and Niagara Falls and the rainforests? What about Mount Everest? What about the Grand Canyon?'

'Yeah,' said Robbie. 'And what about Wembley football stadium? What about Pirate Planet, eh? What about Pirate Planet?'

Opal shrugged happily. 'So show me,' she said.

'Opal,' Martha explained. 'The Earth may seem

like a boring little dot in the universe to you but the fact is it's pretty big. We can't just get in an aeroplane and take you to Egypt or the Amazon. You have to be an adult to arrange stuff like that and you have to have money. Robbie and I can't take you to those places. We can show you pictures of them in a book but we can't take you to them. The most we can do is take you to the end of the road and back.'

Martha expected Opal to look disappointed but she didn't. She jumped to her feet and said, 'Excellent! I've always wanted to go to the end of the road and back. Let's do it!' She snatched Garnet up out of his tin and tucked him into her cape. She flung out her arms and pointed with one finger like a superhero about to begin a dangerous mission. 'To the end of the road and back!' she yelled and began to run a sort of slow motion run, clomping along in her silver boots.

Martha and Robbie looked at one another.

'She's going the wrong way,' said Robbie.

'I know,' said Martha. 'But I guess it doesn't make much difference really.' She flung out her arms and pointed just as Opal had done. Robbie did it too. 'To the end of the road and back!' they shouted and galloped off after Opal.

10

That was the beginning of their days with Opal Moonbaby. Each morning they would make just enough noise in the salon to get Alesha to throw them out into the play area. While Opal gobbled down the food they smuggled for her, they planned their outings.

They never strayed very far from the play area, and they only left it for a short while, coordinating their trips around the length of time Mum would be occupied with each of her clients. If it was a wash, cut and blow-dry she was doing, they had about forty minutes. That was long enough to go to the main road and back. Opal would lean on the hedge and watch the traffic. She always burst out laughing whenever she saw someone on a bike; she liked to run alongside them pretending she was on a bike too. Most cyclists found this rather unsettling and sped

away as quickly as possible. This didn't put Opal off. She thought bikes were a hilarious invention. It was the pedals that did it, the way the riders had to make them go round and round using nothing but their own legs. Opal thought it was madness to waste all that human energy on balancing and pedalling. On Carnelia, she said, all you had to do was *think* of your destination and your sledspangle would take you there in a billisecond.

Sometimes they would haul themselves up on the windowsills of offices so that Opal could see inside. She thought people hunched over computers, or sitting with telephones glued to their ears were even funnier than people on bikes. 'Why do all the males have coloured tails round their necks?' she asked.

'They're not tails.' Martha laughed. 'They're ties!'

'Oh!' said Opal. 'I wish I had one. What are they for?'

'Haven't got a clue,' said Robbie. 'But you can have mine if you like. I never wear it.' The next day, to Opal's delight, he brought his school tie for her and showed her how to knot it. She wore it all the time after that, day and night.

If it was hair extensions Mum was doing or someone was having coloured highlights put in, they had an hour. That meant they could go into the park behind the play area, where they played hide-and-seek in the flowerbeds. They were never able to hide successfully from Opal though, because she always saw right through the tree or the water fountain, or whatever they were hiding behind.

Opal may have been fantastic at seeking but she

was terrible at hiding. She always left a bit of herself sticking out or made too much noise. It was as if she didn't want to stay hidden for long in case she was missing something.

Garnet, on the other hand, was extremely good at hiding. He was so small and flexible, he could tuck himself right inside the thickest bush or the smallest drainpipe, or burrow under a pile of grass cuttings and stay there, so still and so silent that he might as well have been invisible, and Robbie and Martha almost always had to enlist Opal's help to find him. On one occasion, even Opal couldn't find him.

It was the day the window cleaner was washing the windows of A Cut Above. He had nearly finished and was clearing away the last soapsuds, when Martha and Robbie came hurtling out, almost knocking him off his ladder in their haste to join Opal. They had gone straight into the park with her and played three rounds of hide-and-seek. At the end of the third round Opal ran away from them screeching like a peacock, pretending that they hadn't really found her, and they had chased her round and round the broken-down old bandstand until they were all completely puffed out. The three of them were lying on the grass catching their breath and watching the clouds when Opal sat bolt upright and started patting all her pockets.

'Where, in the name of dog, is my mingle?' she said.

Martha and Robbie sat up too and looked about. There was no sign of Garnet. Then Robbie remembered. 'He's still hiding,' he said. 'We forgot to look for him.'

'Well, we'd better find him now,' said Opal. 'Treble quick.'

They searched everywhere, behind every tree, through the flowerbeds, up and down the skateboard park. They even opened the park gardener's hut to check if Garnet had somehow got himself inside that but he wasn't there either. He didn't seem to be anywhere. They called him and called him but he didn't appear.

'Darn it, Garnet,' Opal muttered. 'Where *are* you?'

'But surely you can see him, Opal,' said Martha. 'You always know where he is, even when he's hiding.'

'That's because I always tell him where to hide. He was supposed to be in that lavender bush but he's not there. He must have thought he'd found a better place.' She groaned. 'I feel queasy. I need Garnet back.'

Opal did look very pasty all of a sudden.

'He'll turn up,' Martha said.

'Bound to,' said Robbie. 'It's nearly time for a biscuit. Garnie wouldn't miss biscuit time, not for anything.'

But Opal seemed to be extremely upset. They had never seen her upset before. She wasn't crying or anything but her face had gone very pale. It wasn't white but sort of transparent, like water, and her whole body was trembling. She was gripping her arms with her hands, trying to stop herself from shaking.

'Opal,' said Martha, touching her shoulder. 'What is it, what's happening to you?'

Opal was shuddering so much now that her teeth were chattering and she could hardly speak. 'T-told you,' she stuttered. 'C-Carnelians can't l-last long without their m-mingles. They n-need to be with them at all times or they ex-ex-exp ...'

'Expire?' said Martha.

Opal managed to nod and then staggered and stumbled to the ground.

'What's expire mean?' said Robbie.

'Die,' whispered Martha. It didn't seem real. How was it possible that Opal could be in mortal danger all of a sudden? Only moments ago, she had been messing about and laughing, without a care in the world. And now this. Martha hoped it was just some kind of trick she was playing on them, but one look at Opal's face told her this was no practical joke.

'Robbie,' she said, grasping his sleeve. 'We've got to find Garnet. If we don't, Opal will die.' She stood there gripping him by his shirt, hardly able to believe what she was saying. She knew they had to act quickly but somehow she couldn't move. She was rooted to the spot.

'I'll find him,' said Robbie with surprising certainty. 'You stay here and look after Opal.' Gently, he prised her fingers from his shirt sleeve and ran off, out of the park and down the road, almost as if he knew where he was going. Martha leaned down to comfort Opal, who was beginning to hunch up into a miserable-looking ball.

'Don't worry,' she said. 'Robbie will find him.' She wasn't sure it was true. She stroked Opal's heaving shoulders. 'I didn't know it was this bad,' she said. 'You let Garnet out before, when he brought us to you, on that first day in the flat. You were OK then.'

'D-different,' stammered Opal. 'I t-told him to go. I c-could see him the whole z-zooming time.' She began to cough. 'But he's only supposed to go where I tell him. I have to know exactly where he is and what he's doing. Otherwise I can't . . . can't . . .' She began to gasp for air.

'I understand,' said Martha. 'Don't try to speak any more, Opal. You need to save your energy.' She looked up, anxiously scanning the road for any sign of Robbie, any sign of Garnet. To begin with there was nothing, just a woman pushing a double buggy, a bus sweeping by, the odd passing car. Then she saw him, running like crazy and shouting her name. He had something in his arms and — yes, yes it was — it was Garnet.

'It's all right, Opal,' she said, feeling a sob of relief rising in her throat. 'Robbie's got him. He's got him!'

Robbie raced up, knelt by the huddled figure of Opal and pressed Garnet into her arms. Garnet began licking and licking at her face, the way they had seen him do the first day they had met him. As Garnet licked, Opal slowly straightened up. She stroked Garnet's furry head and her watery skin returned to its normal colour. She was going to be all right.

Martha hugged Robbie hard. She didn't know why but she suddenly wanted to squeeze him and squeeze him. Robbie pushed her away, bending over to catch his breath. 'Thank goodness you found him,' Martha said. 'Where was he, Robbie? How did you know where to look?'

'Window cleaner's van,' panted Robbie. 'I just thought, where would I hide if ... if I was Garnet. He must have got in thinking it was a good place to hide and then ... and then the window cleaner must have shut him in and driven off, cos his van was parked halfway down the road, and I saw him open the back and Garnie was in there, and I ... I got him out and ran back here as fast as I ... could.'

'You were brilliant!' said Martha, clapping her hands together and glancing at Opal again to see if she really was back to normal.

'You *were* brilliant,' said Opal, her loud voice returning to its usual volume. She walloped Robbie on the back. 'Thanks, cucumber hero,' she said heartily. 'You're a gem. Do you know, for a minute there, I thought I'd had my fish and chips!'

Martha stared at Opal. It was unbelievable. One minute she had been at death's door and the next she was idly scratching her stomach like a happy chimpanzee at a tea party. She was asking Robbie what he fancied doing next, behaving as if nothing serious had happened at all. Meanwhile she, Martha, was feeling sick; she thought she might even throw up.

'Opal,' she said. 'We need to talk about this. You've got to be more careful with Garnet from now on. You mustn't let him out of your sight ever again.'

Opal looked at her. 'Ooh, Martha,' she said.

'You've gone green. Your face looks like a scoff capsule that somebody's sucked.'

'Yeah,' said Robbie. 'Or a puddle of melted mint ice cream.'

Martha stamped her foot angrily. 'Will you two please be sensible for one minute? You could have died just then, Opal. Do you understand? You could have died!'

'I do believe,' said Opal, with a sly look, 'that you're actually properly worried about me, Martha. You must be starting to care for me, like a true friend.'

'Never mind about friendship,' Martha snapped back. 'It's got nothing to do with that. You could have died. What do you think would happen to Robbie and me if we were found with a dead alien on our hands?'

'Mmm,' said Opal, pondering the idea. 'I can see that might be a little awkward to explain. Well, I certainly don't want to be a nuisance so I shall make every effort to stay alive and ticking from now on.'

Martha couldn't work out whether Opal was serious or joking. And she couldn't decide whether she wanted to hug her or shake her, or both.

'Maybe you should give Garnet some training,' suggested Robbie. 'Like they do with puppies to make them more obedient.'

'Good idea,' said Opal. 'Garnet,' she said sharply. 'Ankle!'

Garnet went and stood dutifully by Opal's ankle.

'It's "heel" actually,' said Martha. She sighed. At least it was a start.

✳ ✳ ✳

From that day on the four of them, Martha, Robbie, Opal and Garnet, stuck together like glue. Whatever they did, they did it together. They never went anywhere very grand or did anything very extraordinary but that didn't bother Opal. Although she always insisted that everything was bigger and better on Carnelia, she couldn't hide her fascination with Earthly things. Tumble driers in the launderette and parking meters by the side of the road were just as interesting to her as palaces and cathedrals. The lift that went up and down in their block of flats was as thrilling to her as a fairground ride was to Martha. She just loved pressing all the buttons and seeing them light up. Apparently nothing on Carnelia worked like that. There were no buttons to press. You just used your own thought patterns to make things work.

She liked pressing buttons so much that Robbie smuggled out Mum's mobile phone for her to see. He produced it one morning while they were inside the concrete pipe, sheltering from the glare of the sun. He wanted to show her how to play games on it. Opal, however, had never seen a phone close up before and she was much more interested in learning how to key in numbers and how to text. The first thing she did was accidentally call the salon. Martha and Robbie tried to get her to hang up when they heard Alesha saying in her most elegant voice, 'Good morning, you're through to *A Cut Above Hair and*

Beauty, Providers of Complete Head Refurbishments. How may I help you?' Opal had no idea which button to press in order to end the call and she was far too excited to look for it.

'Good morning to you, dear lady,' she bellowed into the phone. 'One moment, please, caller.' She leaned over to Martha and whispered, 'I've learned how to talk Telephone. It's in the Earth Manual. Watch this.' She went back to the phone and said in a singsong way, 'What is the purpose of your call? And whom shall I say is speaking?'

'You what?' said Alesha, not quite so elegant-sounding now. '*I'm* not calling, am I? You rang me.'

'I'm so sorry,' said Opal, grinning at Martha. 'But Miss Moonbaby is not available at the present time. May I take a message?'

'Are you having me on?' Martha heard Alesha say.

Opal looked puzzled. 'Having you on what, madam? Having you on toast, perhaps?'

'I'll have *you* on toast when I catch you,' shouted Alesha. 'I haven't got time for prank callers, now you stop blocking my line. There could be an important client waiting to—'

'Goodbye!' Opal boomed, pressing everything at once and cutting Alesha off.

Martha put her head in her hands. 'I hope she doesn't check the number,' she said. 'She'll have a fit if she finds out that was us.'

'She won't,' said Robbie, tickling Garnet under his chin, the way he liked. 'Alesha's far too busy refurbishing people to bother with that.'

'I hope you're right, but Opal, you'd better give that phone back before you get us into any more—'

Kersnick. The phone flashed and suddenly Martha couldn't see anything. She couldn't see Opal or Robbie or even the walls of the pipe. All she could see was whiteness. A whiteness so bright, so intense, it made her head throb. Sitting squashed in the concrete pipe with that whiteness was like being trapped in a cupboard with a streak of lightning that was trying to find a place to strike. The white beam of light rushed around the pipe, bouncing off the walls, banging into their knees, their elbows, their faces. Eventually it found its way to the end of the pipe and shot out, dissolving immediately in the August sunshine.

Martha and Robbie sat there, unable to speak, so dazzled that all they could see now were purple splodges floating around in front of their eyes.

'Oops,' said Opal. 'Sorry about that, Earthlings. I think I must have found the camera setting. I'm not supposed to do that. The Earth Manual says if you find a camera you have to get away from it quickly. You have to treat it like a hot tomato.'

'Hot potato,' said Martha.

'What's so bad about cameras?' asked Robbie, rubbing his eyes.

'For one, there's the light thing which might attract a bit of attention,' said Opal. 'And for two, there's the photo itself. How are we going to get rid of this?'

She turned the phone screen towards them. The purple splodges in front of Martha's eyes changed to pink and then faded away altogether and she could see again. She looked at the phone and gasped.

'What . . . what's that?'

'That,' said Opal, 'is the real me.'

Opal had taken a picture of her own face but it didn't look like the Opal they knew. The face in the picture was different. The eyes were still violet with bright-blue centres but they were massive, completely out of proportion with the rest of her face. They practically filled the screen, like a pair of planets, and as Opal turned the phone from side to side, the eyes seemed to shift and to move. Different colours began to appear in them. Turquoises, ochres, silvers and greens circled and chased one another across their surfaces like deep swirling waters of ever-changing skies.

'That's what I look like on Carnelia.' Opal took a closer look at the photo. 'Ahh,' she crooned. 'Reminds me of home, sugary home!'

'Wow!' sighed Robbie, stroking Garnet's ears. 'That's awesome! Why can't you be like that all the time?'

'Because people might notice, of course,' said Martha. 'If Opal had come here looking like that she'd have been arrested straight away. She'd probably be in some scientist's lab by now, being poked and prodded about.'

'Like she was ET, you mean?' said Robbie, his own eyes goggling. 'Or something out of *Dr Who*?'

'Precisely,' said Opal. 'Which is why we need to

dispose of this photo forthwith.' She began thumbing through the phone's menus. 'Where's the Neutralise-and-Obliterate button?'

Martha hastily grabbed the phone from her. 'Let's just stick with deleting it, shall we?' She took one last look at the photo of Carnelian Opal. She already believed Opal was an alien, but if she had had any doubts, this photo would have been all the proof she needed to dispel them. She clicked the dustbin icon. 'All gone,' she said. She put Mum's phone away in her pocket. 'I think that's enough excitement for one day. How about we go and look at Opal's poster instead?'

'Ooohhh goody!' said Opal. 'I love my poster.'

They crawled out of the pipe and went over to their usual place on the pavement and sat down.

Opal adored all pictures, but there was a huge poster by the bus stop on the opposite side of the road which she found particularly fascinating. The poster was advertising handbags. In it, a handbag was dangling on a long golden chain and a man and a woman were standing on top of it, clinging to one another as the handbag appeared to swing to and fro against a background of an exotic beach, palm trees and the ocean. Opal could sit in front of that poster for hours. As far as Martha could gather, they didn't really go in for artwork on Carnelia. Opal said they didn't need it. They already had a dazzling galaxy, a whole raft of stars and the entire Silky Way to look at. The view on Carnelia was so good, she said, that to try and distract Carnelians from it with simple drawings or paintings would have been pointless. Still, her eyes were continually drawn back to the handbag poster. Looking at it seemed to make her happy.

When Martha asked her why she liked it so much, she said, 'Can't put my thumb on it really. It's something to do with the way the Earthlings are looking at one another. Like they each think the other one is a rare bird they've just spotted.'

'They're meant to be in love,' Martha explained.

'Oh yes, love,' said Opal dreamily. 'I've heard of that. There's something about love in the Earth Manual. I didn't know that's what it looked like though.'

'If you think that's good,' Robbie told her, 'you should try the cinema or go to a football match, where things actually move. I bet you'd love watching telly.'

Opal disagreed. 'Oh no, if I want entertainment I just pick up my swimbat and go to the fantarium,' she said.

'Is that a swimming pool?' asked Martha as a bus drew up, blocking their view of the poster.

'No,' said Opal. 'It's a wind pool. Much more fun. There are all these different coloured winds swooping in at you and you have to use your swimbat to bat them away really fast. Each type of wind has its own home and you have to send it flying into the right one. Like this.' She stood up and started whacking imaginary winds with her imaginary bat. 'No wind can escape *my* swimbat,' she said. 'Gales, gusts, tempests and tornadoes, I can beat them all into place.' She scooped ferociously at thin air. 'Look at that! Oh yes, Opal Moonbaby strikes again. Right on target, every time!'

'What's the target like?' said Martha, remembering that she still had some unanswered questions. 'Is it like the target in your challenge? The one in Part Three of your Carnelian Independence Award?'

But Opal never seemed to want to talk about her challenge. 'What?' she said, stopping her batting. 'No, it's got nothing to do with the CIA. Nothing at all. Oh, look, the bus is going. We can see our handbag again.' And with that she settled down on the pavement for another twenty minutes of poster-watching.

When they weren't going on outings they sat by the paddling pool or in the concrete pipe, looking at books and talking. Martha brought a book called *Your Amazing World* which was full of colour photographs of mountain ranges, deserts and waterfalls. She wanted to prove to Opal that Earth was really a wonderful place. Opal did look at the photographs for a while but she was more fascinated by the book itself. She relished turning over the pages and smelling them, smoothing down each one with her palm. 'Look at those lovely black letters, all in neat little rows,' she marvelled. 'How do you train them to do that?'

'Come on, Opal,' said Robbie, who wanted her to hurry up and turn the page so that he could see the next picture. 'Anyone would think you'd never even *seen* a book before.'

'I haven't,' said Opal, pressing her face into the pages. 'Not nose to nose, anyway.'

'Not even when you were small?' asked Martha. 'Don't you have books on Carnelia? Did no one ever read you a story?'

'*Stor-y*' said Opal slowly, savouring the word. She flickered her eyelids. '*A narrated chain of connected events*. No, I don't think I've ever heard one of those. What are they like?'

So, one by one, Martha brought her favourite books to the play area and read them aloud to Opal and Robbie and Garnet. They had fairy stories and Greek myths, African legends, and *Tin-Tin* and *The Jungle Book*. Opal liked *Alice in Wonderland* best because of all the getting big and small that Alice did. Garnet preferred *Puss in Boots*. They knew he liked it because every time Puss did something clever, he would stand up on his hind legs in the cake tin and show his claws and go *yip-yip-yip*.

Martha loved reading the books to Opal. She and Chloe had read books together when they were still friends and they had read the funny bits and the sad bits out to one another. That was one of the things that Martha missed most since Chloe had gone off with Colette. Whenever she thought of Chloe and how close they had once been, she felt that cold dinner-plate weight in her stomach again, but it wasn't quite so heavy now, or quite so cold.

11

One hot afternoon they were lounging together on the big basket swing while Martha read. Opal was lying flat on her back putting drops into her eyes with a dropper. At the same time she was blowing bubbles with her own saliva, a trick Robbie had taught her. Garnet crouched on her chest, flicking out an occasional paw to burst the bubbles as they appeared in Opal's mouth. Robbie was sitting up and rocking the swing to and fro while his monkey did acrobatics on his lap.

Martha was just getting to the exciting bit, where the heroine of the story had to ride in the good giant's pocket, keeping completely silent so as to avoid being captured by the bad child-eating giants, when Opal suddenly said, 'Oh no you don't!' She scooped Garnet into her arms, jumped off the swing and dived into a nearby wheelie bin.

Martha and Robbie looked around, wondering what had made Opal hide. There didn't seem to be anybody about. Martha thought it might be something to do with the story until she saw a man in the distance, walking towards them. As he came closer she recognised him.

'The milkman,' she said under her breath.

'Correct,' said Opal from inside the bin. 'The milkman with a camera. A camera with a flash.'

'That's bad,' said Robbie.

'Very bad,' said Martha.

'That *is* bad,' came Opal's muffled voice. 'And that's putting it wildly. If he gets a shot of me and my eyes, he'll go straight to the newspapers. I'll be an overnight international sensation.'

'But Opal,' said Martha, 'how does the milkman know what you look like in a photo? The only photo of you on Earth is the one we took on Mum's phone and we deleted that.'

'Ah, yes, well,' said Opal. 'I was meaning to tell you, actually. I had a little difficulty with my landing gear on that first night and I was so busy sorting it out that I forgot to transmogrify on impact.'

'Transmogrify?' said Robbie.

Opal opened the lid of the wheelie bin a fraction. 'Change,' she said.

'You mean ... he saw your eyes? Your real Carnelian eyes?'

'Yes,' said Opal. 'He would have seen them in his headlights.'

'Wow!' said Robbie.

'Is that what made him crash into the tree?' said Martha.

'Yes,' said Opal.

'Oh, Opal!' said Martha. 'That poor man.'

Opal saw Martha's look of sad disapproval and let the lid fall shut again. 'All right, all right, I know,' she said from inside the bin. 'Big mistake. It's my fault. Anyway, now this milkman thinks all he has to do is take my sunglasses off and my Carnelian eyes will be revealed for all to see. Which is wrong. But he also thinks if he gets a photo of me he'll be able to prove to everyone that I'm an alien. Which is right.'

'Because the camera will change your eyes to Carnelian ones?' said Robbie.

'Exactly. And if he gets his little snap of me looking like that I'll be public property. Then I can kiss goodnight to my Carnelian Independence Award, the Moonbabies will risk losing the Carnelian Coronet and Uncle Bixbite will blow his tops.'

The man was almost in earshot now. If Opal didn't stop talking she was going to give the game away.

'Quiet!' Martha whispered. 'He'll hear you!'

'Yes, sir, Mr Madam!' Opal hissed back. She always had to have the last word.

Sure enough, the man was looking for Opal. He must have recognised Martha and Robbie from the day in the mini-market because he came straight over to them.

'Hello, you two. Where's your alien friend, then?' he said.

'Pardon?' said Martha as innocently as possible. 'I'm not sure . . .'

'Don't you go trying to make a monkey out of me,' the man cut in. 'You know who I mean.' He began fiddling with the camera, turning it over in his hands and pressing all the buttons. 'The Martian girl with the hair and the pooch.'

'Martian? I don't think we know any Martians, do we, Robbie?' She wasn't lying. Opal didn't come from Mars, she came from Carnelia.

'Definitely not,' said Robbie, watching the man struggle with his camera. 'By the way, you've got that the wrong way round. You're taking pictures of your stomach.'

'Oh,' said the man, hastily tucking in his shirt. 'Thanks. I've just borrowed it from my cousin actually. When I catch up with that alien I'm going to take a nice big photo of her with this camera. I don't know where she's from, Mars, Jupiter or Neptune, but she's not of this world and I'm going to prove it.'

'How do you know she's not?' asked Martha.

'Not what?'

'Not of this world.'

The man tapped his nose with his finger. 'If you don't know then maybe you don't want to know,' he said mysteriously. 'Maybe you don't want to ask what's going on behind those dark glasses of hers. But I'll tell you this, I saw what I saw, and what I saw was not normal.'

'Well,' Martha began. 'We're all different, aren't we?'

'Yeah,' said Robbie. 'What's *normal* anyway?'

'*Who's* normal?' added Martha.

'Who *wants* to be normal?' said Robbie.

The man didn't seem to have heard. 'The other night, see, if she was a human I would have run her over for sure, squashed her flat. There she was, right in front of me and then suddenly, there she wasn't! She must have got beamed up or de-materialised or something. I'm sure of it. I'm going to prove she's an alien. Then everyone'll see I'm not crazy.'

'I'm sure you're not crazy,' said Martha, who didn't want to be unkind. 'But I'm afraid we don't know where Op— I mean we don't know where that girl is now.'

'Yep. Can't help you, I'm afraid,' said Robbie, tossing Yoyo in the air and catching him.

They hoped the man would go away then but he didn't. He looped the camera strap over his shoulder and sat down heavily on the bottom of the slide.

'I don't want everyone thinking I'm barmy,' he said, more to himself than to them. 'Barmy people can't get girlfriends. There's this lovely girl, Tina she's called, works at the depot. I was just getting ready to ask her out. She was going to say yes too, I'm sure of it, and then this happens and I get the sack. Now they're all taking the mickey, Tina thinks I'm off my trolley and today I hear she's going out with Marcus from Quality Control. Marcus!' He shook his head. 'How could she go out with that loser?' He kicked despairingly at the bark chips.

'I'm sorry,' said Martha. She couldn't think of anything else to say.

The man stared at her. 'You ought to be careful, you ought,' he warned. 'Mixing with aliens. You never know what trouble they might bring with them, you don't.'

'What do you mean?' asked Martha. 'What sort of trouble?'

'Who can say? She's brought trouble to me all right. I've lost my job. Everyone thinks I'm off my rocker. But I'm not. I know a thing or two about aliens. You can't trust 'em, for one thing.'

There was a stifled squawk of indignation from the wheelie bin.

'What was that?' The man frowned.

Robbie squawked too and then cleared his throat. 'Sorry,' he said. 'I've got a bit of a cough. How do you know you can't trust aliens?'

'Well,' said the man. 'Stands to reason. They're not human, are they? Intelligent, yes. But honest? Or reliable? I don't think so.' Warming to his subject, he stood up and leaned an elbow on the wheelie bin. 'No, if you know what's good for you, you'll keep away from that alien girl. Aliens are no good! You can't trust 'em as far as you can throw 'em.' A sudden outraged jerk of the wheelie bin dislodged his elbow and he almost fell over. 'What the heck?' He put up a hand to lift the lid.

'Sorry,' Robbie said quickly. He flung himself off the swing and sprawled on top of the bin, pressing the lid down firmly. 'It's my ... my dog.

He's having a rest in there. You must have woken him up.'

A high-pitched barking came from inside the bin.

'Funny sounding dog,' said the man, becoming suspicious. 'Let's have a look at him.'

'No can do,' answered Robbie. 'He's dead fierce, especially when he's just been woken up.'

'That's right,' said Martha. 'And he's a very big dog.' Immediately the barking became louder and deeper. 'We wouldn't want him to bite your ears off or anything.'

'Mm. Big fella, is he?' said the man, stepping back nervously, his hands cupped over his ears as if to protect them from slavering jaws. 'Well,' he said. 'Anyway, you tell your friend when you see her, I know what she is and I'm going to prove it. One photo, that's all I need. Just one photo.'

The barking became even louder but the man still seemed reluctant to leave. Martha racked her brains for a way to get rid of him. 'You know what,' she said, looking at the camera hanging down from the man's shoulder. 'I bet you'd be a really good photographer, if you practised a lot.'

'Really?' The man looked surprised, pleased even.

'Yes,' said Martha. 'You've . . . you've got the right build.'

Robbie snorted. Martha gave him the warning look.

'Do you think so?' said the man. 'I didn't know there was a right build for a photographer.'

'Oh yes,' said Martha, amazed that the man was taking her seriously. 'But you need to take pictures of things as well as people.'

'What kind of things?'

'Well, bowls of fruit and trees and ...' Martha caught sight of a straggly-looking daisy that had fought its way up through the bark chips. 'And flowers. Most people start with flowers apparently.'

'Flowers? Do they?'

'Yes, they do. And I don't know if you've been to the town hall recently, but they've got loads of flowers in their window boxes right now. You should go down there and have a look.'

Opal must have got tired of being a dog because the barking changed to roaring and the bin began to jump from side to side.

The man moved away hurriedly. 'Town hall, you say.' He nodded at Martha. 'I'll give it a try. Thanks for the tip.' He set off down the road. 'Remember what I said,' he called back to them. 'Beware! Beware of aliens!' He scurried down the road checking behind him now and then to make sure he wasn't being pursued by a huge, angry dog.

Once the man was safely round the corner Martha and Robbie lifted the lid of the wheelie bin to find a very smelly Opal with an upturned yoghurt pot on her head. Garnet emerged too, sporting an empty crisp packet over one ear. He was holding an egg shell in his paws and happily licking out the runny remains of the egg inside.

'Cheek of the man!' Opal declared, pulling a

rotting lettuce leaf out of her nose. 'Fancy going round bad-mouthing aliens like that. We're not bad. Not the Moonbabies of Carnelia anyway. We're no trouble at all, not like the Mercurials. He should try meeting one of them on a dark night. They'd have his guts for starters! I don't know. It's an insult to the name of Moonbaby, that's what!' She shook her fist at the distant milkman. 'That cheeky donkey! Why, I ought to box his bottom!'

Robbie dissolved into giggles at the idea of Opal boxing the milkman's bottom but Martha was thoughtful. She felt sorry for the man and she wondered if there was a grain of truth in what he had said. Were aliens untrustworthy? Could she rely on Opal?

'What?' cried Opal, reading Martha's thoughts. 'Of course you can. You can trust me inside out and outside in. Your secrets are safe with me, Martha.'

Martha looked at her sharply. 'What do you know about my secrets?' If she could tune in to her mind, maybe Opal already knew her innermost feelings, her most private worries. Perhaps she already knew what had happened with the Secret Circle. Perhaps she knew all about Colette and Chloe and how mean they had been to her.

'Nothing at all,' said Opal. 'Don't worry, I won't read your most personal thoughts. I promise you that.' She stood to attention and solemnly waggled her ears. 'On my Carnelian honour, I promise never to drop eaves on the deep secrets of your mind.'

'Oh,' said Martha. 'Good. No eavesdropping. That's a relief.' Although in a funny way it wasn't. She had often thought about telling someone, Mum probably, about the way Colette and Chloe had treated her. Somehow, though, she had never been able to get the words out. Just the thought of it all made her feel so sad and brought such a lump to her throat, it seemed better not to mention it to anyone. But keeping it all inside was an effort and although the cold dinner-plate feeling in her stomach had faded, it was still never very far away. If Opal had known all about it without Martha having to tell her, that might have made it easier. She thought she wouldn't have minded talking about it then. As it was, she simply couldn't even begin to say anything.

'No,' Opal went on. 'I'm going to wait until you tell me your secrets yourself because that'll be proof.'

'Proof of what?'

'Proof that you're my friend, of course.'

'Oh,' said Martha. 'That.'

'Yes, that,' said Opal, hopping from one foot to the other. 'Come on, we must be friends by now, mustn't we? After all the things we've done. After all the time we've spent together. Robbie's my friend, aren't you, Robbie?'

'Sure am,' said Robbie, sneezing happily as he combed Garnet's coat with his fingers, making sure it was free of eggshells and coffee grounds. 'I've been your friend for years.'

'No you haven't. We've only known Opal for a few weeks.'

'But that's long enough, isn't it?' said Opal. 'To make a friend of someone. I mean, don't you like me, Martha? Don't you like me even a little tiny weeny tinsy bit?' She made a pouting expression, lifted her sunglasses and fluttered her pale eyelashes.

Martha laughed. 'It's not that I don't like you, Opal. It's just that I don't need any friends. I don't *want* a friend.'

'Oh, but, Martha, can't you break your rule, just this once? Just for me? It's not as if I'm even here for very long. Ascendance Night is coming up, you know, and I'll have to go home. Two quakes of a lamb's tail and I'll be gone.'

'What is Ascendance Night exactly?' asked Robbie.

'It's the night I go back to Carnelia, when I'm supposed to have completed my challenge and I can claim my CIA. I ascend on the night of the Earth's next full moon. On your twenty-sixth of August to be precise.'

'That's the same night as the Pirate Planet Fiesta,' said Robbie. 'We're not going though, worse luck.'

'The twenty-sixth,' said Martha. 'That's only one week from now.'

'Exactly,' said Opal. 'One week and I'll be gone. Will you miss me, Martha?'

'I hadn't really thought about it,' said Martha honestly. It was actually a bit of a shock. The twenty-sixth was so soon. And things would be very different without Opal around, that was for certain.

'Oh, say you'll miss me, Martha. Say you're my friend. Go on.' Opal screwed up her face pleadingly. 'Pleeeeaase?' Even Garnet joined in, standing on his hind legs and performing a little begging dance.

It was tempting to say yes. Martha could almost imagine herself walking along with Opal, their arms linked, sharing thoughts, trading secrets. But then another picture slipped into her mind, a picture of Chloe standing with Colette above her on the steps at school. And then another of them jeering at her in the mini-market.

'No,' she said abruptly, shaking away the hurtful images. 'Sorry, Opal. But I can't. I just can't. Sorry.'

'Oh, piddlestitch!' said Opal, looking defeated for a second and then perking up again. 'Well, I'll just have to work harder. I can tell you're going to be a tough nut to track. I'll make you change your mind somehow, Martha, you'll see. I'll start tomorrow.'

But they didn't see Opal the next morning, because everything changed.

12

It was the rain that did it. It came down thick and fast, surprising the dry ground, gushing off the rooftops, rushing down the drains. The sky was dark with heavy-looking clouds. It rained hard and it kept on raining.

They couldn't go out to the play area. Mum wouldn't allow it. And Alesha refused to have them in the salon all day long. They had proved themselves far too noisy for that. So Mum made a couple of quick phone calls. A few minutes later Zack and his mum came to the salon to collect Robbie for the day. Then Mum told Martha to put on her rain jacket and wellies so she could walk her round to Chloe's house.

'You don't mind going to Chloe's, do you?' said Mum. She pulled Martha towards her so she could share the shelter of her umbrella. 'I don't know what's

gone wrong but you were such good friends the two of you, surely you can patch things up somehow.'

Martha doubted it. She walked with her head down, dragging her feet through the puddles. 'I'll be fine,' she said.

'Only, I can't really think of another option. Not while this rain lasts anyway. Come on, love,' Mum said, squeezing her arm. 'Whatever it is can't be all that bad, can it?'

'I'll be fine,' said Martha again, drawing away from Mum and pushing her fists deep into her pockets. She tried to look on the bright side and think about how kind Chloe's mum was, how much she liked Chloe's house, her garden and the pond. Maybe Mum was right, maybe things wouldn't be too bad.

'Good news, Martha,' said Chloe's mum, as she greeted them at the door. 'Colette's coming round too.'

'Really?' said Martha, feeling slightly sick.

'Yes. As soon as Chloe told her you were coming she said she wanted to come too. So the three of you can have lots of fun together.'

'Great,' Martha tried to say but her voice wouldn't come out properly and she ended up coughing instead.

'You're not getting ill, are you?' said Mum.

'No, of course not.' Martha wished Mum would stop asking her things. 'You get back to the salon. I'll see you later.'

She went into the house and hung up her coat.

Chloe was standing at the foot of the staircase, her arms folded in front of her.

'Hi,' she said, without smiling.

'Hi,' Martha answered. They both stood there awkwardly, not knowing what to do next. Martha thought how much she'd rather be at the play area with Opal and Robbie. Even in the pouring rain it would have been miles better than this.

'So, what do you want to do?'

Martha shrugged. 'Dunno. You?'

'Nothing much.'

It wouldn't have been like this before. When they were still friends. Before, they would have been bubbling over with ideas of how to spend the day. They would have both been talking at once, spilling out suggestions, saying exactly the same thing at the same time, and laughing. Not any more.

'Oh, hi there, Chlo-Chlo! Sorry I'm *sooo* late!' Colette brushed past Martha as if she was invisible and gave Chloe a long hug. 'I was absolutely *dying* to get here earlier,' she simpered. 'But my dad just took *forever*! *So* annoying!' Then she turned to Martha, pretending she'd only just seen her.

'Oh, hello,' she said coolly. 'Heard we had to babysit today.' She slipped her arm through Chloe's. 'Come on, Chlo,' she said. 'Let's go up to your room.'

Martha hung back, stroking the polished wood of the stair rail. She didn't want to go up to Chloe's room at all. But she couldn't spend the whole day at the bottom of the stairs or Chloe's mum would realise something was wrong. She had no choice but to follow them.

They were huddled over the desk when she went in, whispering and giggling over Chloe's diary. They ignored Martha completely. She sat down on the end of Chloe's bed and looked around the room. Last summer it had been full of inviting clutter, boxes of interesting toys all jumbled together, and the walls had been covered with posters of animals. Now the toys were gone, making room for a dressing table which was littered with jewellery and make-up sets. The animal posters had been replaced with photos of the pop stars and footballers that Colette said were good-looking.

'Where's Stomper?' said Martha suddenly, remembering Chloe's floppy-eared bunny who had always sat on the beanbag next to her bed.

'Stomper?' said Chloe. 'Oh, he's gone.' Martha thought she looked a bit wistful.

'Long gone,' said Colette firmly. 'Chloe gave him away to the school jumble sale. We're not into soft toys in the Secret Circle. I sent all mine to the dump ages ago.'

'But don't you miss him?' Martha asked. 'I thought Stomper was your favourite toy? A present from your granny?'

'She doesn't miss him a bit, do you, Chlo?' said Colette.

'No, not a bit,' said Chloe, rather quietly. 'We're too old for that stuff now.'

'I couldn't give away a special toy like that,' said Martha. 'Not ever.'

'Exactly,' snapped Colette. 'And that's why *you're* not in the Secret Circle any more.' She gave Martha a mean little smile, put a possessive arm round Chloe and went back to poring over the diary.

Martha sat on the bed plaiting and re-plaiting the tassels on Chloe's blanket while the other two gossiped about school, about the other girls in the Secret Circle and about the costumes they were going to wear for the Pirate Planet Fiesta at the end of the summer holiday.

'We can go as damsels in distress,' said Colette. 'They've got these gorgeous long dresses in the costume hire shop. With ribbons and masses of fake pearls sewn on all over. I'm going to have the green one, to match my eyes, and you'd look lovely in the pink. It would really set off your complexion. We'll look like twins!'

'Amazing!' said Chloe. 'I can't wait! I bet you're going to win the fancy dress prize, Col.'

'No, Chlo, I think you will. You're going to look *sooo* beautiful.'

'No, it's bound to be you.'

'No, I think you.'

Martha felt completely left out listening to all this but even so, she couldn't suppress a chuckle. It wasn't really even a chuckle, more of a little puff of air escaping out of her nose. But Colette noticed it immediately and pounced.

'I don't suppose you'll be going to the Pirate Planet Fiesta, Martha.'

'Probably not this year,' Martha admitted.

'Why's that then?'

'My mum's a bit busy.'

'Couldn't your dad take you?' Colette said innocently. Although she knew perfectly well, like everyone else at school, that Martha's dad wasn't around now. Martha didn't answer. 'Of course the tickets are really expensive,' Colette carried on. 'Dad said it cost him an arm and a leg but he doesn't care. He'd do anything for me.' She sat back and folded her arms. 'Pirate Planet'll probably drop the prices next year. Once they've been open for a while. Maybe you'll be able to go then, Martha.'

Martha looked at Chloe, who hastily looked away. She was the only person Martha had ever told about Mum's money worries. She had obviously gone and told Colette. How *could* she?

'Anyway,' Colette went on nastily. 'What do you care? You're not interested in getting dressed up or looking good, are you? You said so yourself.'

'Yeah,' Chloe whispered, but loud enough for Martha to hear. 'She still likes puppies and cute kittens.'

'Right,' answered Colette. 'I bet she still plays with those stupid toy animal families!'

Martha clutched at her little shoulder bag, which actually did contain a small family of squirrels she had brought with her to pass the time. There was no way she was going to get them out now. She carried on plaiting the blanket tassels.

Colette laughed. 'What's the matter, Martha? Did you forget your baby blanket or something?'

Chloe brought out some chewing gum and offered it to Colette, who took a piece and said, 'We'd give you some, Martha, but you're a bit young for chewing gum. We don't want you accidentally swallowing it, do we?'

'I'm the same age as you,' Martha retorted.

Colette looked at Chloe and smirked. 'Yes, but you don't act it, do you? You're really immature. You need to grow up a bit. Now put your dummy in, and keep quiet!' She and Chloe sniggered together and started reading each other's horoscopes out of a magazine that Colette had brought with her.

Martha wanted to shout or to cry. Most of all she wanted to run down the stairs and beg to be allowed to go to home. But if she insisted on going back to the salon, Alesha might give Mum the sack. She didn't want to risk that. So she made herself get up and go to the bookcase. She went over there like a robot, chose a book at random and sat down. She tried to read but the words made no sense and kept blurring over, as her eyes were watering a bit.

She found herself thinking about Opal instead. She wondered what Opal had done once she'd realised she and Robbie weren't coming to see her that morning. She would probably be hungry. Would she decide to go off and explore by herself? Martha hoped she would be all right. She wished she could be with her. Because someone ought to be with her. If only to keep her out of trouble.

13

It stopped raining after lunch and the three girls went out into the garden. Chloe and Colette wanted to go back upstairs but Chloe's mum said they needed some fresh air. Martha was relieved to get out of the house and went straight over to the pond where she and Chloe had spent so many lovely hours last summer. Chloe showed no interest in it now, even though there were pond skaters dashing about all over the surface. She and Colette huddled together on the bench.

Under the water, a newt paddled to the side and Martha scooped it up in her palm. Opal would like this, she thought, they probably don't have newts on Carnelia.

'No newts, no frogs, no toads,' said a voice. 'No salamanders, no mud-puppies and no water-dogs. No amphibians at all, unless you count the Mercurials, of

course. They can live on land or in water and they're just as mean in both places.'

'*What* on *Earth* is *that*?' said Colette.

Martha turned to see Opal sitting on a postbox overlooking the garden. She was completely drenched. Her clothes were plastered to her long arms and legs. The brim of her hat was heavy with rainwater. She was perched there, hugging her cape round her bony knees, like some huge damp bird.

'Opal!' said Martha. 'I was just thinking about you.'

'I know!' Opal chirruped. 'And in answer to your questions, I was a bit miffed when you didn't come but then I decided to follow you and that cheered me up. I was hungry but I've eaten three raisins I found in my pocket, half a bun I found in a bin on the way here and a woodlouse I found crawling up my leg – not tasty.'

She stood up, leaped off the postbox, her cape flying out behind her, and landed in the flowerbed, right by the bench where Colette and Chloe were sitting.

'Oh yes, and I haven't got into *any* trouble. Have I, Garnet?' Garnet jumped out of Opal's pocket, shook himself vigorously as if in answer, and then began to dig in the soil. Opal shook herself too, showering the bench with water. 'No trouble at all!'

'Well, you're in trouble now!' said Colette, getting up, hands on her hips in outrage. 'How dare you come barging into my friend's garden without even being invited? How dare you let your dog, or

134

whatever it is, do his business in her flowerbed?'

Opal laughed. 'Don't be silly,' she said. 'Garnet isn't doing any business. He's a pet, not a businessman.' She bent down and gave him a pat.

Colette looked baffled for a moment. 'Whatever,' she said. 'But you do realise this is private property? You're trespassing!'

'Am I really?' Opal replied with great interest. '*Trespassing*,' she savoured the word. 'What's trespassing? Sounds like fun.'

'It's not a *good* thing,' said Chloe. 'As a matter of fact it's a crime!'

'Yes,' said Colette. 'We ought to call the police.'

'Oh, don't do that,' said Martha quickly. 'Opal doesn't mean any harm. She's just come to see me, that's all.'

'You?' said Colette, narrowing her eyes. 'Someone's come to see you? Well, that *is* a surprise.'

'What's so surprising about it?' Opal asked.

'Well,' said Colette, 'I don't want to be mean, but . . .'

'Yes you do,' Opal interrupted.

'What – what did you say?' Colette faltered.

'You do want to be mean,' said Opal. 'That's exactly what you want.'

'No I don't,' Colette insisted. 'Anyway, what would you know about it? You only met me a moment ago. I'm just saying that Martha's not exactly the most popular person in the world.'

'No?' said Opal. 'Who is, then? Is it the Queen, or the Pope? Or Father Christmas? No, don't tell me.

135

I know this one. It's Henry the Eighth.'

Colette frowned. 'I'm saying that Martha's not the most popular person at school, that's all.'

'Why the devilled eggs not?' demanded Opal.

'Well,' Colette went on, 'not that it's got anything to do with you but she's a bit babyish, that's all. Into little kids' things still. Teddies and that kind of stuff.'

'Yes,' Chloe said. 'It's nothing personal. It's just the rest of us have moved on from all that now.'

'That's right,' said Colette with satisfaction. 'We've got a more mature outlook on life. No offence.'

'Oh, I get it,' said Opal slowly, as if the truth was just beginning to dawn on her. She pointed at Colette. 'So *you're* the most popular person in the world.'

Colette shrugged, trying to look modest. 'Not in the world, but in the school perhaps.'

'I see!' Opal fondled Garnet's ears. 'The others all look up to you because you're so sophisticated. But . . .' She put a finger to her chin. 'There's one thing puzzling me. Don't they mind about Mr Tickle Bump?'

'What?' said Colette, looking shocked. 'What did you say?'

'Who's Mr Tickle Bump?' said Chloe.

'Haven't you told her about him?' asked Opal innocently.

Martha thought Colette looked almost nervous. 'I don't know what you're talking about,' she said.

'Yes, you do,' said Opal. 'Mr Tickle Bump. You're thinking about him right now, aren't you? He's your ickle dickle teddy weddy and he's got his own little nappy and he goes to bed with you every night. In fact you can't sleep without Mr Tickle Bump, can you?'

Colette went very white and then very red.

'Is that true?' said Chloe, with the beginning of a frown. 'You told me you gave all your toys away. Do you really have a teddy to go to sleep with still, a teddy with a nappy on?'

'And a dummy,' Opal added. 'With a blue silk ribbon on it.'

Colette was practically purple now. 'No!' she spluttered. 'Of course it's not true. She's making it up. It's a load of rubbish. I've never even met this person in my life so how could she know anything about, about . . .'

'Mr Tickle Bump,' Opal reminded her. 'He's got a zip-up bottom, remember? You can keep things in there. You wouldn't forget him in a flurry, would you? Not your cutie wutie little boywoy?'

'No!' cried Colette. 'I mean yes. I mean, there's no such thing. Don't listen to her, Chloe! She's making it up!'

Opal wasn't making it up at all. She was reading Colette's thoughts. Not very wisely, in Martha's opinion. Not if she didn't want to attract attention to herself and make people suspicious. But Opal never seemed to act wisely. She always did things as soon as she thought of them. She was grinning at Martha now as if to say she knew she wasn't being sensible but she simply couldn't resist it. She looked as if she was warming up to say something else, something that would embarrass Colette even more, but then quite suddenly she picked Garnet up out of the cat-mint plant he was rolling in and said, 'Well, I've loved our cosy little chat but I'm afraid I must fly now, because you have another visitor.' With that she slung one long leg over the fence, followed it with the rest of her body, and went hop-scotching off down the street.

'Chloe!' called Chloe's mum through the window. 'Come and see who's just popped in.' The girls were all looking in the other direction, gazing after the person who had just popped out. Chloe's mum came into the garden. 'Come and say hello to cousin Barton, Chloe.'

Chloe put her hands up to her face. 'Oh no, not my cousin again! He's so annoying!'

'I know,' said Colette, who seemed relieved by the distraction of the new arrival. 'He was here last week. What a loser!'

'He was bad enough before he lost his job,' said Chloe. 'But now he's unbearable!'

Martha was shocked to see the ex-milkman shambling over the lawn towards Chloe, a half-eaten biscuit in one hand and the camera in the other. Now she understood why Opal had made such a speedy exit. So *this* was Chloe's cousin Barton. She had heard her talk about him before, Martha remembered, about how he was looking for a girlfriend and how irritating it was that he always helped himself to the biggest slice of cake, but she had never met him. She sidled quickly back to the pond and knelt down, pretending to look for tadpoles. She didn't want the man to recognise her. Luckily he didn't seem to notice her as he was so keen on talking to Chloe.

'Thanks for lending me this camera, Chloe,' he said. 'It took me a while to get used to it but I think I've really got the hang of it now.'

'Oh,' said Chloe. 'Great.'

'Yes, as a matter of fact, I think I might be a bit of a dab hand at this photography thing. I took a lot of pictures of my own feet and my tummy button to start with but now I've got some really good shots. Still-lifes and close-ups and so on. Petunias, geraniums, you name it. I've got eight hundred and seventy-three pictures of the same dandelion, actually. All taken from different angles. Would you and your friend be interested in seeing a slide show?'

There was a pause. From her place by the pond Martha imagined Chloe and Colette looking at one another, grimacing probably. Then Chloe said, 'Sorry, Barton, Colette and I have a homework project we need to get on with.'

'Oh, all right then.' Barton sounded disappointed. 'Some other time maybe.' His voice brightened. 'I'm quite busy myself actually. You see I haven't got the photo I want yet. There's just one photo I need to get. It's a photo that's going to change my life, it's going to make people really want to know me. That's why I came over, to see if I can hold onto your camera for a bit longer. Would you mind, Chloe?'

'No,' said Chloe. 'It's fine. Keep it as long as you want.'

Martha knew what photo Barton was talking about. It was the one of Opal. The one he was following them about for. He wasn't going to give up until he had his proof. Martha shivered. She remembered the severity of Uncle Bixbite's voice when he had warned Opal about the serious consequences of failing her CIA. Martha didn't know what those consequences were but she didn't like the sound of them. She didn't like the sound of the Mercurials either, the clan from Carnelia that Opal said kept their power in their hair and could live on land or sea. She didn't think it would be a good idea for them to win the Carnelian Coronet. They might do all sorts of terrible things, maybe things that would even affect the Earth. She felt sure it would be much better if the Moonbabies kept hold of the Coronet.

She could hear the man going back towards the house with Chloe. He was still talking about the camera and how he was going to enter some kind of photography competition. It sounded as though he wanted Chloe to ask him more about the competition but she didn't say anything at all. When Martha heard the door close behind them she straightened up, brushing at her knees, which were damp and muddy. She turned and saw Colette standing there, staring at her.

'Strange friend you've got.'

'What?' said Martha. 'Opal, you mean? Oh, she's just someone I met.'

'Where?' said Colette.

'What?'

'*Where* exactly did you meet her?'

'Just around and about,' Martha answered as vaguely as possible.

'Well, there's something pretty weird about her if you ask me,' said Colette, who had now almost completely recovered her super-cool exterior. 'And her dog, if it *was* a dog. Never seen one like that before. It could be an illegal breed. Where's she from, anyway? She's got a really funny way of speaking. Funny clothes too. Where does she live?'

'Quite . . . nearby,' said Martha, beginning to feel rather unsettled. Colette was the last person she wanted to find out about Opal's secret home in the ground floor flats. She held out a hand, palm upwards. 'Raining again,' she said. 'Think I'll go in.'

But Colette seemed determined to find out as much as she could about Opal and she quizzed Martha about her for the rest of the day. How old was Opal? Where did she go to school? What was she doing, out and about on her own? Who was supposed to be looking after her? If she lived nearby, why had Chloe and Colette never seen her before? By the time Martha went home she felt as though she had been through some kind of heavy-duty police interrogation. Her head was swimming. She didn't think she had given anything important away but she still felt distinctly uneasy.

M artha couldn't stay worried for long though. She kept thinking about the look of shock on Colette's face when Opal came out with the truth about Mr Tickle Bump. Opal had seen straight through those two and their mean ways and she had known exactly how to get under Colette's skin. The way her jaw had dropped when Opal described her teddy bear down to the last detail! Martha smiled every time she thought about it.

'It's good to see you looking a bit more cheerful these days,' Mum said. It was one of her rare Saturday mornings off and she was still in her dressing gown. 'More than we can say for your brother, I'm afraid.'

Robbie was banging about noisily in his bedroom. 'He's all upset,' explained Mum, 'because Zack's been to Pirate Planet again. But guess what? I've got a surprise for him. I've been doing quite nicely at A

Cut Above the last couple of weeks and Alesha's giving me a raise. What with that and the tips I've been getting, I reckon we can afford to go to Pirate Planet after all.'

'Oh, Mum,' said Martha. 'That's fantastic! Robbie's going to be so excited.'

'I thought we could go on the fiesta day, you know, when everyone dresses up? And you can each bring a friend. Robbie'll ask Zack I expect, even though he's been fifty million times!'

'Fifty million and one,' Martha reminded her.

They laughed and then Mum said gently, 'Is there a friend you'd like to invite, Martha?'

Martha was about to say no, there wasn't, and she'd rather go just as a family when a thought came to her. Not a thought so much as a picture. It was a picture of Opal and her, sitting together in a roller coaster car, laughing, Opal's luminous hair streaming out behind them like a silken sunshine against a blue, blue sky.

'Actually,' she said slowly, 'I suppose there might be a . . .' She stopped. She had almost said it. She had almost said the forbidden word. 'There might be – someone – I could ask.'

'Brilliant!' said Mum, and she went to give Robbie the good news.

Martha sat very still, thinking. Was it really going to happen? Was she really going to make friends with Opal? She didn't know. She didn't even want to know. All she knew at this precise moment was that she couldn't think of anything she'd rather do than go to Pirate Planet with Opal Moonbaby. The Fiesta at Pirate Planet fell on the same date as Opal's Ascendance Night, when she was supposed to return to Carnelia having completed her challenge. Martha realised she wasn't ready for Opal to go home yet. She wished she could stay right till the end of the summer but if she had to go, Martha couldn't do anything about it. At least if she came to the Fiesta, they'd be able to give her a really good send-off.

The banging in Robbie's room came to a halt. There was a short silence, then a squeal of joy and Robbie marched out of his room singing his Pirate Planet song at the top of his voice, swinging Yoyo in front of him as he went.

'Pirate Planet! Pirate Planet!
It's a date!
Pirate Planet! Pirate Planet!
I can't wait!
Pirate Planet! Pirate Planet!'

He picked up two saucepan lids and began clanging them together like cymbals. Mum, trying to make herself heard above this triumphant noise, told Martha she was nipping to the salon to give Alesha back the hair magazines she had borrowed.

'Pirate Planet! Pirate Planet!
Pirate Planet! PIRATE PLANET!'

Martha jumped up. 'I'll do it for you,' she shouted over Robbie's din. It was the perfect excuse.

'You don't have to, love,' Mum shouted back. 'You see enough of the salon as it is.'

'I don't mind,' Martha yelled happily. She grabbed the sheaf of magazines, ran past Robbie who was still singing his song, which now had bonus features:

'Fi, fi, fi, fi fiesta! Pirate Planet!
Fi, fi, fi, fi fiesta! Pirate Planet!'

and was out of the door. She didn't wait for the lift but instead went clattering down the four flights of stairs. She ran into A Cut Above, plonked the magazines on the reception desk, gave a quick wave to Alesha and rushed straight out again and over to the entrance to the ground floor flats.

But she found her way blocked by Colette, who was coming out of the flats with Chloe.

Martha stopped. 'What are you two doing here?' she said, panting.

'Might ask you the same question,' replied Colette. 'These flats are out of bounds. My dad says so. He *is* the caretaker round here, you know.'

'I know,' stuttered Martha. 'I wasn't – I mean I was just looking for – for Robbie.' Martha didn't want to mention Opal, or Colette would be forever snooping around. Maybe she was snooping around already.

'Well, he's not here,' said Colette. 'We would have seen him. We've just been through the entire place.'

'Oh,' said Martha weakly. 'Have you? Thanks.'

Colette and Chloe sauntered off. 'By the way,' Colette said over her shoulder. 'If you're looking for that freaky friend of yours, we saw her not long ago, in the kiddie playground over there. Why don't you go and find her? You can be toddlers together!' She laughed and then she was gone.

Martha ran for the play area. She still had time, just about. Mum wouldn't be missing her yet. She couldn't wait to see Opal's reaction when she told her about the trip to Pirate Planet. 'Zippedee-do-dogs!' she would say, or 'I'm pickled pink about that!' She would jump for joy and Garnet would *yip yip* and run round them in circles.

Opal wasn't in the play area. Martha checked inside the pipe. There was no sign of her. Martha was wondering whether to give up and run home when she noticed a strange mauve haze drifting over from the paddling pool. Going to the fence, she saw Opal sitting on her haunches at the water's edge, deep in conversation with the rippling underwater figure of Uncle Bixbite. Martha ducked down and peered through a knothole in the wood.

'Time is running out, Opal,' Uncle Bixbite was saying. 'You do realise that? If you don't complete Part Three of your challenge by the next full Earth moon, you won't get your CIA and you know what the consequence of that will be.'

'I know,' Opal replied, reaching up to stroke Garnet who was curled around her neck, sleeping. 'I'll be banished and have to spend a whole year on Earth in exile, and the Moonbabies might lose the Carnelian Coronet. But don't worry, Uncle Bixie, the Moonbabies are more than a match for the Mercurials and there's no way I'm going to stay on this tiny pellet. If I was stuck on Earth for a whole year I'd probably go stark raving bananas. And what's more, Part Three's almost sorted. She's going to fall for me any day now, I can tell. I'll be back home in a squiffy.'

'I think you mean a jiffy,' said Uncle Bixbite. 'I hope you're right. I hope this child is the right one. I wouldn't like to see you waste a whole year of your life on this antique of a planet. It's well past its sell-by date.'

'Can't happen,' said Opal confidently. 'Martha's definitely the right one. The Datatron always identifies the correct target. It's very reliable. I wouldn't be surprised if she was on her way to find me right now. She'll declare her friendship and be eating out of my handkerchief in no time!'

'You're sure?'

'You bet I am. As sure as legs is legs!'

'Very well,' said Uncle Bixbite, seeming reassured. 'Then I shall make plans for your Ascendance to Carnelia.'

'See you on Ascendance Night, Uncle Bixie,' said Opal cheerfully.

'Vatengpaxxz!' they both said together and Bixbite disappeared with a hiss of steam. The mauve haze evaporated and Opal stood up to leave. She went humming along up the bank towards the fence as if she didn't have a care in the world.

It was a warm day but Martha felt herself shivering all over. She went hot and then suddenly cold. Her teeth were chattering so loudly in her head, she felt sure Opal would hear, but for once Opal, whose humming had now turned to a merry whistling, didn't notice Martha crouching by the fence. She hurdled straight over it and began to walk away, towards the flats. Martha slowly got to her feet. Her legs felt trembly, as if they wouldn't support her. Her mouth was dry and she felt sick but she had to speak.

'What's a Datatron?'

Opal stopped in her tracks and turned round. 'Martha?' she said, smiling. 'How's everything going?' She stuck out her arms and pointed to the ground with both index fingers in the way Robbie had taught her. 'How's it dangling?'

'It's not "how's it dangling?"' said Martha. 'It's "how's it hanging?" and stop trying to change the subject. I asked you a question and I think you owe me an answer. What exactly is a Datatron?'

'Oh, that,' said Opal.

'Yes,' replied Martha. 'That.'

Opal nodded. 'You heard, then?'

'Yes,' said Martha. Her lips felt tight across her mouth. 'I did.'

'Then I suppose I'd better spill the greens.'

'I think you'd better.'

Opal took a deep breath and said quickly, 'A Datatron is a bit like your computers, only cleverer. You put in the coordinates of anywhere you're going and it tells you everything about that place, however far away it is. About the lie of the land, the type of people, the wildlife, the history, where the shops are, the drains, the mouse holes, the anthills. Everything really.'

149

'And it identifies targets?'

'Yes.'

'Targets like me?'

Opal looked her steadily in the eye. 'Yes.'

'So what you're saying is that you decided to make friends with me because my name came out of some, some lucky dip machine! You've spent all this time trying to convince me to be your friend, not because you liked me or liked the look of me or anything but because some great big metal robot said you should. Just so you could win some stupid award!'

'That is how it began,' Opal confessed, an unusual look of worry crossing her face. 'But then I really started to like you, Martha. For yourself, I mean. I do like you. You're the best. A real star-quality girl. I think being an Earth friend with you would be fantastic.'

'Too bad!' spat Martha. 'Because that is never going to happen. You can forget your CIA award or whatever it's called because I will never *ever* be your friend! I promise you that! I don't care if you never pass your challenge. I don't care if I never see you again. In fact, I really hope I don't. Even the sight of you makes me feel sick. I hate you, Opal Moonbaby! I absolutely hate you!'

She realised she was shaking now. Shaking from head to foot. Tears of anger began to well up in her eyes. Before they could overflow, she turned and ran as fast as she could, back to the flats and away. Away. It was all she could think of. She had to get away.

Martha lay on the floor in the storeroom of the salon. She rested her cheek on the cool tiles. They felt solid and comforting and she wanted to stay there forever.

What a fool she had been. After all the promises she'd made to herself never to make another friend, she had almost gone and got involved all over again. Why hadn't she learned her lesson? She had made friends with Chloe, and Chloe had betrayed her. She had almost made friends with Opal, only to discover that the whole thing was just a horrible trap. And she had been about to walk right into it. Why couldn't she have kept her promise? Well, never again. She screwed her eyes shut. *Never never never again!* The milkman was right. You couldn't trust aliens. You couldn't trust anyone.

'Opal's on the pipe,' said Robbie, who had his

nose pressed to the window. 'She's calling your name.'

'Let her,' said Martha.

'In fact she's shouting it.'

'Not interested.'

'I know,' said Robbie. 'We're not going to see her any more. Not after the way she tried to trick you. We're going to stay well away.' Martha had told Robbie about the Datatron and the way she had been selected as a target. He thought a Datatron sounded really cool and wished he could have a go with one, but Martha had been so upset that he had agreed not to talk to Opal, for a while at least.

Robbie began sorting through a pile of temporary tattoos, trying to decide which ones to use for the Pirate Planet Fiesta the following evening. 'Thing is,' he said, 'Opal's going back to Carnelia tomorrow night, isn't she?' He looked out of the window again. 'She's waving her arms around like mad. She wants us to go out there. We haven't been for days now.'

Martha picked at a flake of paint on the skirting board.

'We ought to say goodbye, don't you think? It would be rude not to.'

The flake of paint came away. It was dry, like paper.

'She looks quite hungry, actually. Upset too. Do you think maybe we should forgive her now?'

Martha crumbled the paint in her fingers and let the crumbs fall to the floor.

'Oh, look,' said Robbie. 'I've just found half a slice of toast in my pocket. How did that get there? The jam side's got a bit fluffy but it would still taste OK.

Especially if you were really hungry.' He scratched his head. 'Hey! Maybe Opal would like it.'

'You'd better not be an actor when you grow up, Robbie Stephens. You'd be terrible at it.'

Robbie grinned.

'If you want to go and see Opal that's up to you,' said Martha, propping herself up on one elbow. 'But I'm not coming with you.'

Robbie stuffed the toast back in his pocket and jumped over Martha's outstretched legs. His hand was already on the door handle when he stopped and said, 'I'll just go for a bit, OK? And I won't be very nice to her. I'll make sure she knows how we feel.'

'Fine.'

He waved his monkey. 'I'll make Yoyo bite her ankles for you.'

'Fine.'

Robbie shot out of the door and Martha was alone. She sank down and gently drummed her fingers on the floor tiles. Now at least she could have a bit of peace. She let her eyes close. She might even be able to go to sleep. She liked being asleep. You didn't have to think when you were asleep.

'Ay caramba! What are you doing down there, Martini? I nearly tripped over you!'

'Sorry,' said Martha, rubbing her eyes. 'I was just looking for, for something.'

'Looking for something indeed! Having a nap, more like,' said Alesha, though not unkindly. 'Come on, Martini, stop moping in here and make yourself

154

useful. Your mum's gone to the wholesale suppliers for more hair products so I'm on my own out there. And I've a young lady client who wants a hot chocolato. You can do that for me, can't you?'

'Yes,' said Martha, standing up and straightening her shirt. 'Sure.'

'Good,' said Alesha, clicking her fingers. 'Make it snappito then, if you don't mind.'

Martha enjoyed stirring up the hot chocolate and spraying a swirl of cream on the top. She sprinkled over some chocolate shavings and took the drink into the salon, carrying it carefully so that the cream didn't flop into the saucer. But when she saw the young lady client, she froze. *Not her. Please. Anyone but her!*

Colette was sitting in a chair with a magazine she had brought, and she was showing Alesha a photo of an elaborate hairstyle with a whole big mess of ringlets and curls and ribbons.

'Can you copy that?' she asked. 'I want to look exactly like that for the Pirate Planet Fiesta tomorrow night.'

Alesha frowned at the complicated style. 'Hmm. Bit of a tall order, darling, but I'll see what I can do,' she said. 'It could take a while though.'

'Take as long as you need,' said Colette.

Martha forced herself to move forward, keeping her eyes fixed on the hot chocolate. Colette smirked as she put the drink down in front of her. 'Oh thanks, Martha,' she said. 'Allowed to use the kettle now, are you? Aren't you grown up?'

Martha ignored her and headed for the storeroom

but Alesha told her to stay at the reception desk. She wanted her to answer the phone while she got on with Colette's tricky hair-do.

So she had to sit listening to Colette prattling on to Alesha about what *great* friends she was with Chloe and how they had a *fantastic* club at school but that she couldn't tell Alesha *anything* about it because it was *top secret*. Colette wouldn't have been talking about the Secret Circle at all if she hadn't wanted to make Martha feel bad. She didn't realise Martha felt bad already. She couldn't feel any worse than this. Colette might as well have saved her breath.

'My very best friend Chloe and I are going to the fiesta as twin sisters,' she said. 'We're going to be damsels in distress.' Colette kept glancing at Martha in the mirror but Martha wasn't rising to the bait.

Then something happened which really made Martha sit up and take notice.

'Oh, look,' said Colette pointedly. 'There's my dad. He's clearing out all that stuff the squatters left behind.'

'Squatters?' said Alesha. 'What? In the flats? I didn't know about them.'

'No one did,' said Colette, crossing her legs and nestling herself deeper into the chair. 'I was the one who found out, actually. I saw all this stuff piled up in one of the empty flats. It was a right mess. Really dirty too. Of course, I told my dad about it straight away. He's the caretaker of the flats, you see.'

'I see,' said Alesha, stopping to stare at all the things being brought out and dumped into a waiting skip.

'Looks like you've done us a favour there, darling. Rubbish like that always attracts rats sooner or later.'

It wasn't rubbish. It was all the things that Martha and Robbie had brought Opal, to make her life on Earth easier, to make her comfortable. Cushions, and a lamp Opal had loved but couldn't actually use because the flat had no electricity, some flowery material, an old calendar, a blanket, a picture of Niagara Falls, and Garnet's cake tin. It wasn't rubbish at all. And the only rat it had attracted was Colette. This was her revenge. Ever since Opal had said that thing about Mr Tickle Bump, she had been determined to get her own back. But this was much worse than anything Opal had done to her. All because of one little remark she was breaking up Opal's home, robbing her of a place to stay, all her belongings, everything. It was the meanest thing in the world. And there was more.

'What's that he's got, wrapped up there?' said Alesha. 'Looks like a baby.'

'It's some sort of dog thing,' said Colette. 'I told Dad about that too. He's going to take it to the dog pound this afternoon. I think it's an illegal breed. It'll get put down, I expect.'

She hopped out of the chair, went over and opened the salon door, giving Martha a triumphant glance as she passed. 'Hi, Dad,' she called. 'How's it going?'

'Oh, hello, precious,' the caretaker called back. 'Thanks for the tip-off. You were right about the doggy, been abandoned probably. Vicious little tinker, isn't he? Tried to bite me. I'm going to take him home and shut him up until we can get him to the pound.'

'Good for you, Dad,' said Colette. 'I'll see you later, I'm just having my hair done.'

'Righty-ho, pet,' said her dad. 'You're going to win that fancy-dress competition, easy.'

Colette swanned back to her seat and Alesha carried on coiling little tresses of hair up on the top of her head.

Martha was left looking at Garnet. Or the bit of Garnet she could see. His nose was just sticking out of the blanket he was swaddled up in; it was twitching wildly and his eyes were dark and wide open. He was frightened.

Martha watched for as long as she could, craning her neck to see, as Colette's dad strode off with the stricken mingle in his arms. He went towards his bungalow by the main entrance to the block. She saw him go inside, shutting the door behind him.

Martha stood stock still. Ice seemed to thread itself through every single one of her veins as she recalled what Robbie had said earlier. Opal was standing on the pipe, he said, waving her arms about and looking upset, shouting Martha's name. Opal hadn't been asking for company or forgiveness, as Martha had thought – she'd been asking for help. That had been over half an hour ago. Now Garnet was a prisoner and Opal was alone without her mingle. She couldn't survive much longer without him. Without Garnet, Opal would die.

In the distance, the salon phone began to ring.

'Get yer phone, Marphini,' Alesha said through teeth full of hair grips.

Martha didn't move.

'Yer phone!' Alesha said again.

Robbie rushed in. 'Martha!' he gasped. 'It's Opal!' Seeing Alesha and Colette, he dropped his voice to a whisper. 'She's going grey. She's all floppy and she's breathing funny. She's just lying there in the pipe. Garnet's disappeared. I don't know what to do! Martha! Tell me what to do!'

Martha came to her senses. 'Answer the phone.'

'What?'

'Stay here and answer the phone. I'll deal with this.'

She flung open the door and ran out. Behind her, hair grips clattered to the floor, Alesha called, 'Oi! Where do you think you're going?' and Robbie

gabbled into the phone, 'Hello-A-Cut Above-Hair-and-Beauty-how-may-I-help-you-what-do-you-want?'

She couldn't let this happen. She had to get Garnet back. She didn't know how, but she was going to do it. She had to. It didn't matter what Opal had done to her. She didn't deserve this. She didn't deserve to die. No one did. If Opal died ... Martha's heart trembled at the thought. If Opal died she would never forgive herself.

She ran straight through the estate, her flip-flops smacking on the tarmac, until she reached the back of the caretaker's bungalow. Immediately she began checking for an open window, rushing from one to the next. Maybe she could climb in and release Garnet without being seen. It was no good; all the windows were shut and locked. There was no way in.

She couldn't give up. From Robbie's description it sounded as though Opal was fading fast. She thought of the day when Garnet had got himself trapped in the window cleaner's van, how quickly Opal had fallen ill, coughing and dropping to the ground almost immediately. Now she was sick again and all alone in the concrete pipe. Dying alone, maybe. Sudden hot tears rushed into Martha's eyes. She rubbed them away at once with the heels of her hands. She couldn't cry now. She had to stay calm. She had to find another way in. She dashed back round to the front of the bungalow, to Colette's front door. Swallowing her nerves, she rang the doorbell.

She had no idea what she was going to say.

After what seemed like hours, Colette's dad answered. He was drying his hands on a towel.

'Hello, young lady. What can I do for you?'

'I, I'm from the salon,' she stammered, resisting the urge to push past him and begin her search right away. 'Colette asked me to come. There's a magazine – with a hairstyle she's wants. She forgot it. It's . . . in her bedroom!'

'Hair magazine, is it?' said Colette's dad. Martha had never heard anyone speak so slowly. 'I wouldn't know about that. Girls' stuff, that is. Tell you what, why don't you go through to her room and find it? You'll have a much better idea of what you're looking for.' He gestured along the hall: 'Second on the left.'

'Thanks,' said Martha, stepping inside. She made herself wait until Colette's dad was safely in the kitchen and then tiptoed down the hall, trying all the doors. She found the bathroom first, and then a big room with a double bed and an exercise machine in it. There was no sign of Garnet.

The next door she opened was Colette's. Desperately she swept the room with her eyes but one glance told her that Garnet wasn't here either. Mr Tickle Bump was, though. She recognised the teddy bear immediately. He was tucked up like a little king on Colette's frilly pillows, complete with nappy and dummy on a blue ribbon, just as Opal had said. No wonder Colette's eyes had nearly popped out. But Mr Tickle Bump was only a teddy. Garnet was a real live mingle and she needed to find him. Now.

She left Colette's room and stood in the hall, listening. The kettle was hissing away. Colette's dad would be out of the kitchen before long. Water was sloshing to and fro in a washing machine somewhere. There was another noise too, barely audible, but definitely there. Martha squeezed her eyes shut, trying to hear better. There it was again, a whining sound coming from the back of the bungalow. She padded softly along the hall until she came to one last door. She put her fingers on the handle.

'Found what you were looking for, have you, love?'

She froze. Caught.

She whipped round but Colette's dad was only calling from the kitchen. She could hear the chink-chink of a spoon as he stirred his tea.

'Um, nearly,' she called back, her voice quivering with the effort to sound normal. She pressed down the door handle and slipped inside.

It was a tiny room. Nothing in it but a cupboard, a washing machine and a wash basket. The basket was pressed against the machine, which was in full spin and making a squeaking, whimpering noise.

Since when did washing machines whimper? Martha took a closer look at the basket and realised that Garnet was in there, still wrapped tightly in a sheet. She'd found him. He couldn't move his paws or wings. He was trussed up like a bit of meat ready for the oven. And he was absolutely terrified. He was staring at the spinning drum of the washing machine, as if he thought it was a monster about to devour him in its rotating jaws.

Martha smiled with relief. She knelt down and touched Garnet's head, making him jump.

'It's all right,' she said, stroking his soft ears. 'It's all right, Garnie. You're safe now.' Although she knew he wasn't. Yet. Working quickly, she began to unwrap him, unwinding the sheet until he was free. She held his warm little body to her; he was shuddering. 'Don't worry, boy. I'll get you out of here.' But how? She couldn't very well stick him under her shirt and walk out of the front door with him. Colette's dad was bound to notice. Garnet was small but not that small. She had to think of something else.

She peered round the door. Colette's dad was still in the kitchen. He had the radio on and was shouting out the answers to a quiz. 'No! 1992, you idiot, it was 1992! Oh, give me strength!'

Clutching Garnet to her, Martha ran back into Colette's bedroom, looking for something, anything, in which to hide the trembling mingle. A box, or a bag, or – a bear! She plucked Mr Tickle Bump from the bed and turned him over. Yes! He had a zip, just as Opal had said. Martha undid the zip, pulled out Colette's lacy pyjamas and flung them at her pillow.

'Sorry, Garnie,' she said, pressing him into the space left by the pyjamas. 'It won't be for long, I promise.'

Garnet didn't want to go inside Mr Tickle Bump. Every time she got him halfway in, he reversed back out again. She tried putting him in tail first but that was even harder. At one point he almost burst free from her arms, and even tried to spread his wings and flap away from her. She grabbed him back just in time.

'Garnet!' she said in a fierce whisper. 'You have to go in. It's the only way. You have to!' The mingle was so upset, he didn't seem to understand. He just rolled his amber eyes at her in anguish. Martha felt terrible handling him so roughly, forcing him to do something he clearly didn't want to do at all. But if she was to have any chance of saving Opal's life she had to get Garnet inside Mr Tickle Bump, and she had to do it now. Finally she pushed him in sideways, tucking his legs under him, and tugged quickly at the zip. It was a tight squeeze and Garnet squeaked when she got his fur caught in the teeth of the zip, but she managed to free him and finally fumbled the zip shut. She tucked Mr Tickle Bump under her arm, grabbed a magazine from the pile by Colette's bed and ran for the front door.

'Oasis!' Colette's dad was saying to the radio. 'The band was Oasis! Honestly, why do these dummies phone in at all?'

'Got it,' she called, as she sidled past the kitchen, keeping Mr Tickle Bump as far out of sight as possible. 'Got the magazine, thanks, bye!'

She was almost at the front door when the quiz finished. Colette's dad switched the radio off and came out of the kitchen. 'Right-ho, love. I'll get the door for you.'

'Oh, don't worry,' said Martha. 'I can do it.'

He was already undoing the latch. 'What've you

got there then?' he said, indicating Mr Tickle Bump's ears which were sticking out from behind her back. Slowly, Martha brought the bear out. She could feel the warm weight of Garnet inside. His little heart was beating rapidly against hers, which was pounding almost as fast. She wasn't going to be able to reunite Garnet with Opal, she was going to have to hand him over to Colette's dad. Her plan had failed and Opal was going to die. She clutched Garnet to her as if he was the only warm thing left in the world.

'Oh, she wants her little Mr Tickle Bump, does she? I don't know! She doesn't like to be parted from that teddy for long. Time she grew up, I think, but you try telling *her* that.'

Garnet was beginning to wriggle inside the bear. 'Yes,' said Martha, trying to keep him still. If she could just prevent Colette's dad from realising the mingle was in there, they might still have a chance. 'Well, I'd better take him over to the salon now.'

'She tells him all her secrets, you know,' Colette's dad went on. 'All the things she doesn't want her dear old dad to find out!'

Martha attempted a laugh, as she took a firmer hold of the writhing pyjama case and edged towards the door. But Colette's dad was getting into his stride.

'Mr Tickle Bump does everything with her. Watches TV, has tea, he's got his own crockery, dinky little spoon and everything. And do you know,' he said, laughing, 'he's even got a voice box and it goes, "*I want my mama! Change my nappy!*" You press just under his chin. Look, I'll show you . . .' He reached out to press Mr Tickle Bump's voice button, which was precisely where Garnet's nose was. Martha whirled him away just in time.

'Thanks,' she said. 'I've got to go. Maybe some other time.' She almost leaped over the doormat.

'Right you are then. Give my love to Colette.' He gave her a wave and shut the front door.

Martha let out an enormous sigh. She felt as if she had been holding her breath the entire time she was in there.

There was no time to waste.

She unzipped Mr Tickle Bump just enough so that Garnet could poke his head out, and ran round to the play area. He was obviously feeling much better because he was chiggering and chattering away. Martha could tell he was going on about what had happened to him and demanding to know why it had taken her so long to release him.

'Never mind about that now,' she told him. 'Opal's pining away without you. We have to get you back to her.'

'*Chigga chi chee,*' Garnet agreed, as Martha set off at a sprint, a tiny flame of hope still flickering in her heart. 'Let me be in time,' she prayed. 'Please, let me be in time!'

Opal's boots were protruding from the concrete play pipe, lying splayed outwards, very still. It was hard to tell if there were actually any feet inside them. Martha unzipped Mr Tickle Bump completely and Garnet shot out and ran-flew over the boots and into the pipe. Martha followed. Bending down, she saw that Opal's legs really were attached to her feet inside the boots. She was lying on her back with her eyes closed and her hands folded across her chest, looking very pale. Deathly pale.

Garnet scampered back and forth along Opal's body. He was frantic. Then he stopped scampering and began to lick her eyelids. He licked and licked, all over Opal's face, her ears, her chin. Opal didn't move a muscle or make a sound. Garnet lay down by her head and pressed his muzzle softly against her throat. He looked back at Martha with doleful eyes.

They were too late.

17

Martha's legs suddenly felt as though they had turned to jelly and she put a hand on the concrete pipe to steady herself. The pipe was hard and cold, like a gravestone. Its two occupants lay together, motionless. Martha watched. There was nothing else she could do. As she gazed at the two figures, she heard a thin keening whine. It took her a moment to realise that it was coming from Garnet. It was the saddest sound in the universe.

'She's ... she's dead, isn't she?' Martha breathed. Garnet looked at her and something pale and blue trickled from one of his eyes. A tear drop. Immediately tears pricked at Martha's own eyes. Opal was dead and it was all her fault. If only she hadn't been so wrapped up in her own hurt feelings she could have stopped Colette, warned Opal somehow. Maybe if she'd agreed to be her friend to begin with,

and never minded about being the stupid target, it would have been all right. Opal wasn't really bad, she was just trying to carry out her tasks, that was all. It wasn't Opal's fault the Datatron had picked Martha. Maybe it had picked her for a reason. Maybe it could see she needed a friend. She really did need a friend, she realised, as she stood there feeling so, so lonely. She had needed Opal's friendship all along. She needed it now. But it was too late. Everything was ruined. What would happen to Garnet? How was she going to tell Robbie? He'd be heart-broken. She screwed her fists into her smarting eyes. 'I'm sorry, Opal,' she cried. 'I'm so sorry I let you down!' She couldn't believe it. Opal was dead. Dead!

The leaves of the old copper beech tree began to rustle, as if a strong wind had suddenly got up. *Dead, dead*, they seemed to whisper.

'Dead!' Martha sobbed.

'*Dead, dead!*' echoed the leaves. '*Dead as a doodoo!*'

Martha looked up. 'What?'

'Dead as a doodoo!' said Opal. 'Or is it a dodo?' She opened her eyes and tried to sit up. 'At least I would have been in about five nanoseconds. You got here in the nip of time, Garnet. Any longer and I would have been a goner.'

She fondled Garnet's ears and Martha saw the life flooding back into her pale face. Opal wasn't dead. She was safe. She was going to be all right. Relief washed over Martha like an ocean wave.

Garnet nudged at Opal's ear and whispered and growled rapidly into it. Opal looked at Martha.

'Garnet says you rescued him and brought him back to me. You saved my life, Martha. Thank you.'

Martha felt suddenly embarrassed. 'It was nothing,' she said. 'Anyway, it wasn't just me. Robbie helped too. He raised the alarm.'

'Nothing?' said Opal. 'Nothing? That's the *somethingest* nothing *I've* ever known!' She studied Martha closely. 'But why would you do a thing like that for me? After all, you never want to see me again. You can't stand the sight of me.'

'Couldn't,' said Martha with a small smile. 'Actually I'm quite relieved to see you right now. To see you alive, I mean.'

As to why she had done it, she couldn't say immediately. It had been a gut reaction. When she knew Opal was in danger, she had forgotten about her own wounded feelings. She had forgotten about everything else too. She had just wanted to save Opal.

She wrapped her arms around herself. 'I didn't want you to get the idea that all humans are mean and spiteful. We're not all like Colette.'

'No,' agreed Opal. 'And with friends like her, who needs anemones? Oh, look, you've brought ickle dickle Mr Tickle Bump with you!' Martha realised that she was still clutching the empty bear to her.

'Yes,' mused Martha. 'I suppose we ought to give him back really.'

'Oh yes,' said Opal, taking the teddy from Martha. 'We'll give him back. We certainly will. When the time is right.'

Martha sighed and sat down inside the pipe, next

to Opal. 'You can't go back to your flat, Opal. Colette's dad's completely cleared it. I think they'll have boarded it up by now too. I don't know where you're going to sleep tonight.'

'Right here,' said Opal. She curled herself around the pipe until she was in a ball, her knees touching her nose. She stashed Mr Tickle Bump behind her head for a pillow. 'See! I'll be snug as a bug in a mug!'

Martha was doubtful. 'I suppose it is only for one night. It's your Ascendance tomorrow night, isn't it? You'll be able to go back to Carnelia.'

'No.' Opal shook her head as Garnet sat on her chest and began kneading contentedly. 'Uncle Bixie won't allow it. I haven't achieved all my targets. I won't be allowed back now until the next Ascendance Night.'

'When will that be?'

'Not until six Carnelian moons have done a figure of eight round the Afternoon Star and passed through the Ring of Hercules. Or in other words,' said Opal, stroking Garnet's fur in the wrong direction, the way he preferred, 'I'll have to stay here for four more Earth seasons. Until the next twenty-sixth of your August.'

'Opal,' said Martha slowly. 'Are you quite sure you haven't achieved all your targets?'

'Quite sure,' Opal went on. 'Oh, I know no one's got my photo and I've lived like a normal human being, less or more, but I've completely failed Part Three of my challenge and I'll have to buffer the consequences. I thought I'd mind about that and

173

I do, for Uncle Bixbite's sake more than my own. Do you know what I mind most, though? I mind that you don't like me. You hate me, Martha, and you always will. You'll never be my friend now.' A silence hung in the air between them until Martha said quietly, 'Yes I will.'

Opal didn't seem to hear. 'I understand, Martha. You made a promise and a human being never breaks a promise. I read it in the Earth Manual. It's all there in black and light.' She buried her face in Garnet's fur.

'The Earth Manual's out of date,' said Martha. 'Look at me, Opal. Can't you see what I'm thinking?'

Opal stared up into Martha's eyes. As Martha looked steadily back at her, she saw the colour of Opal's irises brighten and deepen. A slow familiar grin began to spread across her face.

'Yes,' said Opal at last. 'Yes, I jolly well can!' She slapped her thighs. 'I can see exactly what you're thinking, Martha. You're thinking . . .'

Martha cut her off. 'Don't say it, please.'

'Why not, in the name of numb-brains?' said Opal loudly. She was getting really excited now. 'Why shouldn't I shout it from the treetops?'

'Because I don't want to just *think* it,' said Martha. 'I want to say it too.' She tried to stand up but it was too cramped inside the pipe, so she had to make do with kneeling. She lifted her lower leg with one hand and held on to the opposite earlobe with the other. She cleared her throat. 'I, Martha Stephens, do seriously declare that I am Opal Moonbaby's devoted friend. And I swear very, very solemnly that I will definitely be her friend for always and always, whatever happens. It's an absolute promise. No returns.'

'But, Martha,' said Opal, still hardly able to believe the good news, 'why? After everything you found out about the Datatron? The target? The way I lied to you? After all that, how can you still forgive and forget-me-not?'

'I know what you did,' said Martha. 'And it wasn't right. You can't trick people into being your friends, it doesn't work that way, not on Earth at any rate.' She put her hand down to stroke Garnet who had come over and started nuzzling her leg. 'The funny thing is,' she said, 'that none of that seems to matter any more. I like you, Opal. I just do. I like you whatever you do. I can't help it.'

And that was the truth. Martha had been furious with Opal. She had really meant it when she said she never wanted to set eyes on her again. But then, when she'd seen all Opal's earthly possessions being dumped in the street, when she'd seen Garnet being taken away, when Robbie had come rushing into the salon with the news that Opal's life was draining from her, she had realised how much she really cared for her. Perhaps she had cared for her all along, from the very first day. Opal. Dear, funny, quirky, jolly, jumbled-up Opal. Her best and only friend.

'Best and only friend!' whooped Opal, echoing Martha's thoughts. She squealed and stamped her boots on the roof of the concrete pipe above her.

'Best friends!' she yelled. And Martha joined in. It felt so good to say it. 'Best friends! Best friends till the end of time!'

'Keep your voices down!' said Robbie, crawling like a commando into Opal's end of the pipe. 'The milkman's out here. Hello, Opal,' he whispered.

'Hello, cucumber hero,' Opal whispered back happily. 'Thanks for saving my ham.'

'Your bacon, you mean,' Robbie smiled. 'Any time.'

'Shhh!' Martha was peeping out at Barton Green, who was strolling close by. Opal and Robbie shuffled along to join her. He was sauntering along with his hands in his pockets, and he was whistling, not his usual gloomy self at all.

'What's he got to be so zooming merry about?' cried Opal.

'Quiet!' warned Martha. 'He's still got Chloe's camera. If he takes your picture now it'll be in the paper by tomorrow morning and you won't get your CIA. The Mercurials might win the Carnelian Coronet and you won't be able to go home. You'll be trapped on Earth for ages and ages. A whole year!'

'True,' said Opal thoughtfully. 'Too true.' Then she was quiet and the three of them lay there, silently watching Barton Green from the cool darkness of the pipe, three rabbits in a burrow.

When he was safely out of the way, Robbie crawled out of the pipe and stood up. 'Come on, Martha,' he said. 'Mum's at the salon and she's asking where you've got to. We have to get back anyway 'cos I need to work on my costume for the Fiesta fancy-dress competition. I'm going as a mad, seasick cabin boy castaway, with scurvy. And rickets!' He began hobbling around and clutching his throat, making gagging sounds.

'That reminds me, Opal,' said Martha. 'Mum says I can bring a friend to the Fiesta tomorrow. Can you come? Please say you can. We haven't got much time left and I want to spend as much of it with you as possible. Will you be able to come, before your Ascendance?'

'I should zooming well think so!' boomed Opal. 'I'll meet Uncle Bixie's spaceship first and we'll join you there. I like the sound of this fancy dress thing. What shall I come as? A cannon ball?'

Martha and Robbie burst out laughing at the idea of Opal dressed up as a cannon ball and Opal laughed with them. She was always delighted when people laughed at her, whether she was joking or not. She didn't care. The three of them sang a joyful and raucous chorus of Robbie's Pirate Planet song.

'Fi, fi, fi, fi fiesta! Pirate Planet!
Fi, fi, fi, fi fiesta! Pirate Planet!'

Then Martha and Robbie ran off to the salon while Opal blew extravagant kisses after them.

✻ ✻ ✻

'Fancy running out like that!' Mum was hopping mad. 'Alesha was relying on you, Martha, and you just disappeared, didn't even say where you were going.'

'Left me right in the lurcho,' said Alesha huffily. 'And Roberto was no use, he was all fingers and thumbs, and dropping things all over the place.'

'Sorry,' Martha said.

'And where were you, anyway? Whatever were you thinking?'

'Sorry.'

'Is that all you've got to say for yourself?'

Martha shrugged. She couldn't exactly tell Mum what she'd been doing. It was too long a story and she doubted if Mum would believe it even if she did tell her. 'Sorry,' she said again.

That was why she found herself in her bedroom at seven o'clock that night. It didn't feel good, not telling Mum the truth. But even though she was in trouble, Martha felt contented as she snuggled down under the covers, her face warmed by the early evening sun. She was happy for the first time in ages. For once she was really looking forward to the next day of her life.

18

'Where's this mysterious friend of yours, then?' asked Mum as they queued up for candy floss. They had been at the Fiesta for a couple of hours already and there was still no sign of Opal.

'She should be here by now.' Martha looked around anxiously. Pirate Planet was jammed with people, all crushed in, shoulder to shoulder. There was going to be a huge fireworks display at the end of the evening and it looked as though the whole town had turned out to see it. Martha began to wonder if she would ever be able to find Opal in the crowds. She was desperate to see her. All that time she had wasted refusing even to speak to her, and now Opal only had a few hours left on Earth, maybe only a few minutes. Where *was* she? She hoped she wasn't lost.

'Yo ho ho, me hearties!' Robbie bounded over to them, pushing up his bandanna which was slipping

over his black eye-patch. 'Meet the new champion of the Dead Man's Chest. I've just had a virtual battle with Red-Beard, I've sunk his galleon and chopped his crew into tiny little bits. Thanks to me, they're all casualties!'

'How lovely,' said Mum.

'It was,' agreed Robbie. 'And now Calico Zack and me are going to plunder the loot and hoist the black flag on the Slippery Sloop. We're going to be pirate billionaires! But it costs three pounds a go, and I need an extra 50p.'

Mum opened her purse and handed over the money.

'Shiver yer timbers!' Robbie yelled, as he snatched it out of her hand and ran off to find Zack.

'You're welcome,' said Mum. She wasn't cross though. Robbie was obviously in pirate heaven. 'Meet us here for the Fancy Dress Awards!' Mum called after him. Robbie stuck up his thumb to show he'd heard.

Mum bought two sticks of candy floss. They perched on barrels to eat them. Martha flicked her long cat's tail out of the way to sit down and lifted her whiskers so she could eat the sticky spun sugar. She scanned the swelling crowds. There was still no sign of Opal.

'You could have told me you'd changed your mind. We were meant to be sisters!' Colette came by, complaining loudly. She was wearing an enormous pale green dress with puffed sleeves and a voluminous skirt, fluffed out with a load of frilly petticoats.

'And you didn't even do the hair, like we agreed. I had to sleep sitting up all night to keep this looking good, you know.' Colette patted her elaborate curls. Alesha had piled her head high with ringlets and curls running all over the place like little winding rivers. The whole lot was topped off with a flapping green ribbon. 'I hardly slept a wink!'

At first Martha couldn't see who Colette was talking to. Then she realised that Chloe was beside her, almost completely obscured by the billowing green dress.

'I mean, really,' Colette moaned. 'It's not the same with just one of us dressed like this. Why didn't you tell me you weren't going to wear it? You've made me look a total idiot!'

'I'm sorry, Col,' Chloe said. 'I did try it on but it just didn't feel right. It wasn't comfortable. I wouldn't have been able to do anything in it, go on any rides or anything.'

Colette took hold of Chloe's arm. 'You've let me down, Chloe. You've really let me down. I don't know how you're going to make it up to me but you'd better start thinking about that now, or I might just not be your friend any more.'

Colette turned on her high heels and tried to walk haughtily away but one heel got caught in the petticoats, making her stumble. Chloe didn't go after her. She came over to where Martha was sitting. 'Hi,' she said.

'Hi,' said Martha.

Mum said, 'Hello there, Chloe. You came as a cat too, I see. Great minds think alike, eh?'

Chloe looked embarrassed and there was an awkward silence.

'I like your whiskers,' said Martha to break it.

'I like your mask,' said Chloe, relaxing a little. 'I'm in real trouble with Colette. She's furious with me for not wearing the damsel in distress costume. Actually, she's furious all the time at the moment. I don't know what's wrong with her. She says she's lost something but she won't tell me what it is.'

Martha knew what it was. Mr Tickle Bump. Poor Colette. She couldn't tell Chloe about his disappearance because she had promised her that Mr Tickle Bump didn't even exist. And if word got out about Mr Tickle Bump, Colette would be the laughing stock of the entire Secret Circle. Martha wondered what Opal had done with him.

'You going on any of the rides?' asked Chloe.

'Might do,' Martha answered. 'Might go on the Terror of the High Seas roller coaster later.'

'Me too,' said Chloe.

Then Martha caught sight of Opal at last. She was sitting on the steps of one of the temporary toilets, zipping up her big boots. At least Martha thought it was a toilet. It was different from the other cubicles in the row, silvery and sort of egg shaped. She was talking to a man in a royal blue suit, a man with pointy ears. It was Uncle Bixbite. It was the whole of him this time too, not just the front. The full 3D version.

Martha stood up. 'Got to go,' she said. 'My friend's here.'

'Oh,' said Chloe. 'Right.'

'I'll be back for the Fancy Dress Awards, Mum,'

Martha said and she flew off to join Opal.

Opal was dressed in a new silver cloak. Martha thought it must be her travelling cloak. She was also wearing a huge belt with a large silver buckle and long silver gauntlets which reached almost all the way to her armpits. Seeing Martha, she grinned her big-toothed grin.

'Hello, best and only friend,' she said. 'There's someone here you need to meet.'

Uncle Bixbite made his way down the steps of the toilet and shook Martha's hand with his ice-cold one.

'Delighted to make your acquaintance,' he said.

Martha found herself giving a clumsy curtsey. Uncle Bixbite was so tall and elegant, like alien royalty, and she was very nervous in his presence. 'Pleased to meet you,' she managed to say. 'I'm Martha.'

'I know that, Martha,' said Uncle Bixbite, fixing her with his piercing blue stare. He took a brown silk handkerchief from his top pocket and draped it over his wrist. The handkerchief promptly ran up his arm and hung upside down from his ear. It wasn't a handkerchief at all, Martha realised. It was Uncle Bixbite's mingle, a sleek brown bat with eagle eyes and delicate crest feathers.

'Now, Martha,' said Uncle Bixbite. 'I gather you and my niece have become friends.' He said the word 'friends' the way anyone else might say 'cockroaches'. 'Is that correct?'

'Yes,' said Martha earnestly. She didn't want to let Opal down now, so near to her departure. 'Very good friends. The best of friends actually.'

'Excellent,' said Uncle Bixbite. 'Well done, Opal.' He drew her forward. 'This means you have completed your entire challenge. The Carnelian Independence Award will soon be yours and the Carnelian Coronet will remain in the hands of the Moonbabies, safely out of reach of the Mercurial clan. Congratulations. I'm impressed.'

'Thanks!' said Opal. 'I've enjoyed it. As a matter of fact, I've had a crawl!'

'A ball!' Martha said, laughing.

'Yes,' said Opal. 'Thanks to Martha, I've had a ball!'

Uncle Bixbite went on, 'Opal, the time has come to prepare for our Ascendance. We have a long journey ahead of us. Say goodbye to your new friend. It is unlikely that you will ever meet again.'

'Oh, please,' said Martha, panic bubbling up inside her. 'Couldn't she stay just a little bit longer?' She'd only just found Opal and now she was about to be taken away from her forever. She really needed a little more time with her, just one more proper conversation, something she could remember her by. 'Can't she stay? Just for the fancy dress results?'

Bixbite looked severe. 'It's not in the rules of the CIA,' he said. Then his bright blue eyes twinkled and sparked. 'But I suppose a few more insignificant Earth minutes can't do any harm.'

Opal planted a kiss on his cheek. 'Thanks, Uncle Bixie, you're an angel.'

'Yes,' he replied solemnly as they ran off. 'People often make that mistake about me.'

19

As Martha and Opal headed off together, hand in hand, or rather hand in gauntlet, an announcement came over the loudspeakers. 'Please report to the Mainsail stage for the Fancy Dress Awards. Our judges have been touring the park looking for the three most outstanding costumes, and they are now ready to announce the winners.'

'We can't miss this,' said Martha. 'Robbie's desperate to win a prize.' She hurried Opal over to the stage where Mum and Robbie were already waiting with a great many other people. It was too difficult to get close to them but Martha waved to let Mum know she was there.

Two men, dressed as pirate crew, were wheeling out a trolley on which were displayed the prizes for the Fancy Dress Competition. First prize was a gold treasure chest, studded with glass rubies. There

was a large yellow rosette perched on the lid, emblazoned with a big number 1. Second prize was a basket full of Pirate Planet books, toys and souvenirs all tied up with cellophane. Third prize was a toy pirate ship. Sitting next to the pirate ship was a large teddy bear wearing a nappy. One of the men picked it up by an ear. 'Where's this come from, Nev?'

'Search me, Ken,' said the other man. You could hear everything they said because the microphone was on. 'Must be some kid's.'

The man called Nev looked out into the audience and held up the bear. 'Who wants it then?' he said. Lots of children put up their hands. He pointed to a very small girl in a parrot costume and her parents lifted her up onto the stage. She took hold of the bear, which was almost the same size as she was. It had a dummy tied round its neck with a blue ribbon.

'Wait a minute,' said Martha. 'Isn't that ...?' She put her hand to her mouth as a voice wailed, '*Mr Tickle Bump! My Mr Tickle Bump!*' The crowd parted as Colette pushed her way through in her frothy dress, clambered up and grabbed the giant pyjama case from the little girl. The girl yelped and grabbed it back. They grappled together while the two men danced around, not knowing how to separate them. At last Colette wrenched Mr Tickle Bump out of the girl's arms, pulling out some of her feathers as she did so. The girl started to cry.

'Oooh!' winced the man called Nev.

'Nasty!' said the man called Ken, sucking his teeth.

The little parrot's mother climbed onto the stage and started shouting at Colette. 'What do you think you're doing to my daughter?'

'She had my bear,' Colette whined.

'She's four years old! I hope you're proud of yourself.' The woman took her sniffling child by the hand and helped her down. Ken and Nev tutted and walked off too.

Colette was left alone on the stage. Her skirt, which she had squashed between her knees in order to mount the platform, suddenly burst out from between her legs like a pop-up tent. A ripple of laughter ran through the crowd. Her hair-do was a shambles now; the part that was meant to be piled up on top of her head had slipped down and covered most of her face. She looked out angrily, hugging the empty teddy to her. '*I want my mama! Change my nappy!*' it squeaked. The crowd laughed some more, louder this time. '*Change my nappy, change my nappy!*'

Colette picked up her skirts and fled.

'How on Earth did Mr Tickle Bump get muddled up with the fancy dress competition prizes?' Martha said, trying to catch Opal's eye.

Opal was staring at the stage and sucking in her cheeks. It looked as if she was trying not to laugh. 'Search me,' she said. 'I haven't got the fuzziest idea.'

'And if I believe that I'll believe anything,' Martha

replied. 'I suppose Colette deserves it, though. She put your life in danger.'

'She shouldn't have,' Opal agreed. 'But I didn't do it because of what she did to Garnet and me. I did it because of the way she treats you. I saw the way she talked down to you as if you were nothing but a piece of gluing gum, stuck to the sole of her shoe. No one's going to treat my best and only friend like that. It'll do her good to have a waste of her own medicine!'

'Yes,' said Martha slowly, 'but I think she might have learned her lesson now, don't you?' She could see Colette pushing her way back through the crowd, brushing tears from her eyes as she came. Martha almost felt sorry for her.

Opal followed Martha's gaze and winced. 'Ooh dear,' she said. 'See what you mean. I just popped into her mind for a moment and do you know what she's thinking? She's thinking how everybody hates her. Everybody in the whole wide world.'

'I know what that's like,' said Martha thoughtfully.

'I didn't mean that to happen exactly. Have I gone too far?' asked Opal. 'Have I over-egged her pudding?'

'Maybe,' said Martha, smiling. 'Wait here a minute, will you? I won't be long.'

She only had a matter of minutes left with Opal but somehow this seemed important too. She eased her way through the thronging crowd, edging forwards until she was standing in front of Colette, blocking her path.

Colette stopped. The frills on the shoulder of her dress were torn and flopping, and mascara branched its way down her cheeks. 'Oh, it's you,' she said. 'Come to gloat, have you?'

'No,' said Martha. 'I've come to say it was me. I did it.'

'Did what?'

'I took Mr Tickle Bump. I stole him from your flat yesterday, when you were at the salon.'

'I know,' said Colette. 'My dad said you'd been there.'

'You didn't tell anyone I kept him? Not even your dad?'

'I couldn't. He would have kicked up such a stink, everyone would have found out about Mr Tickle Bump. But they know now, don't they?' She gestured at the crowd of people. 'They all know. Thanks to you.'

'I'm sorry,' said Martha. 'That part was a mistake. I'm sorry that happened, Colette. I really am.'

'Well, it's done, isn't it? They'll all be laughing at me for months.'

'I won't,' said Martha. 'I won't make fun of you.'

'Won't you?'

Martha shook her head. 'I know what it's like.'

The two of them looked at each other. Neither of them said anything. There wasn't much *to* say.

Martha caught sight of Chloe who was standing by the candy floss stall, watching them both. 'Chloe's waiting for you,' she said, and she stood back to let Colette pass. As she went by, Martha said, 'See you next term.'

Colette looked startled. Then she said, 'Yeah, OK. See you next term. Bye, Martha.'

'Bye, Colette.' Martha stayed just long enough to see Chloe put her arms round the miserable Colette. She really did look like a damsel in distress now. Martha smiled at Chloe, and Chloe smiled back over Colette's shoulder. Then Martha set off, weaving her way back through the crowd towards Opal.

'Aren't you kind?' said Opal. 'I didn't know you could be so zooming nice to meanies. I'm sure there's nothing about that in the Earth Manual.'

'Colette was mean to me,' said Martha. 'Actually she was horrible to me. I was thinking of telling you the whole story, but I don't need to any more. I'm fine now. I'm stronger than I used to be. Thanks to you.' As she said it, Martha realised that it was true. She didn't think Chloe or Colette would ever be able to hurt her again. She wasn't even angry with them any more. And the heavy cold dinner-plate feeling in her stomach had gone. Gone for good.

Opal looked as if she was about to burst with pleasure and pride. For once, she even seemed to be lost for words. 'Fact is, Martha,' she said at last. 'I'm a bit of a learner driver when it comes to this friendship thing. You see, we don't have friends on Carnelia, not as such, so it's all a bit new to me. But I really want to make a show of it, and I like you so much that when I see you my brain turns to butterflies, and I've been doing a lot of thinking and the thing is . . .'

Opal's words were drowned out by a round of applause. A woman in a big pirate hat had come onto the stage. She introduced herself as Polly Pringle, the owner of Pirate Planet. She began to announce the results of the Fancy Dress Competition. Third prize was awarded to a girl dressed as a ship's biscuit; the biscuit costume was decorated with green mould and had weevils and maggots hanging out of it.

Second prize, to his delight, went to Robbie. The woman said he had been given the prize for managing to cover every part of his body with something piratey. There wasn't one square inch of him that wasn't decked out with plastic daggers, neckerchiefs, gold earrings, bangles, eye patches, temporary tattoos or fake battle scars. Even Yoyo, who was strapped into his belt, was dressed as a pirate. Robbie stood next to the ship's biscuit, happily clutching his basket of prizes.

'Way to hoe! Cucumber hero!' Opal yelled merrily.

'And here's the one you've all been waiting for,' said Polly Pringle. 'First prize for the most original and inventive costume goes to ... the young lady dressed as a twenty-second century space pirate!'

Everyone clapped but no one went up on stage. The clapping continued. No one clapped more enthusiastically than Opal. She loved clapping, it wasn't something anyone ever did on Carnelia. She banged her gloved hands together energetically, not even noticing the woman gesturing towards her, saying, 'Come on, sweetheart, up you come.'

Martha had to give her a hard nudge. 'Opal!' she

said. 'Opal! It's you. They think you're dressed as a space pirate. You've won first prize!'

Opal stopped clapping and looked down at herself. 'What?' she said. 'For this old thing? Oh well, there's no accounting for Earth tastes.' She allowed herself to be led up on stage and she stood next to Robbie, grinning her head off as she was presented with the golden treasure chest.

'What will you keep in there, then?' asked Polly.

'Garnet,' said Opal without hesitation. 'He needs a new place to sleep since someone beetled off with his cake tin.'

'And who's Garnet? Your hamster?'

'Garnet is my faithful and constant companion,' answered Opal. She drew back her travelling cloak to reveal Garnet's furry head sticking out of her inside pocket. The crowd went 'Ahhhh!' He looked so cute tucked in like that. They clapped some more as Opal covered him up again and stood there beaming.

The only person who wasn't clapping was Uncle Bixbite. He was looking very put out about all the attention that Opal was attracting. The sooner she got off that stage, Martha thought, the better.

But now Polly Pringle was ushering someone else onto the stage. 'Ladies and gentlemen,' she was saying. 'We have another winner here this evening. The winner of our recent photography competition. Please welcome our new Pirate Planet Official Photographer!'

'It can't be!' Martha said to herself. But it was.

He was standing proudly on stage. He looked quite

different now. It wasn't just the new smart suit, or the fact that he had had a shave and washed his hair. It was his entire appearance. Instead of looking gloomy and hunted, he looked upright and content. Happy, even. It was a total transformation.

Polly Pringle said, 'Barton here has taken some of the best and most detailed shots of dandelions I have ever seen. As soon as I saw him ... I mean, as soon as I saw *them* ... I knew he was the man for me, er, I mean, the man for *us*.' She glanced at Barton Green with an unmistakeable blush and he blushed too. She cleared her throat and went on, 'What I mean is, Mr Green was clearly the best candidate for the job of Official Photographer at Pirate Planet.'

So the ex-milkman had landed himself a new job and a new girlfriend all at the same time. No wonder he looked different. No wonder he had been whistling so happily when they had spied on him from the play pipe the day before. It was good to see him looking happy at last. Martha was pleased. But she wasn't pleased to see the enormous new camera he had with him, or the extra-large flash gun that was sitting on top of it. If he took Opal's photo with that they'd have the light show of the century on their hands. And as for the photo itself, it would show Opal's eyes in their true Carnelian form. Once that got out, there was no telling what might happen to her.

Sure enough, Barton took a picture of the ship's biscuit girl and the flash went off, bright and white, and the girl was left dazzled and blinking in its wake. Then it was Robbie's turn. He whispered something urgently in Opal's ear. Martha guessed he was warning her to get off the stage, but she didn't respond. She just stood there. It was as if she had no idea what was about to happen.

Barton finished with Robbie and moved slowly towards Opal.

'Get down, Opal!' Martha willed her to listen to her thought. 'Before it's too late!' But Opal couldn't have heard because she gave her a cheery wave. Uncle Bixbite was looking grim, his jaw set firm. Martha thought he might be grinding his teeth. She tried again. 'Opal!' she sent the thought flying towards the stage. 'Opal! This is your last chance. If you blow it, you won't get your CIA and your Uncle Bixbite's going to leave you behind. You'll have to stay on Earth for a whole year. You'll have to do all the boring Earth things. You'll probably have to go to school and have school dinners and do homework. You won't be able to go to the fantarium or ride a sledspangle or see the stars in the Silky Way, not for three hundred and sixty-five whole days. Opal! Do you understand? He's going to take your photo. Your eyes are going to go mad. Get down, Opal! Opal! Can you hear me? Are you receiving me?'

'Proud and clear, Martha!' a voice whispered in her ear. 'Proud and clear!' It sounded like Opal's voice but it couldn't be, she was too far away; she was still standing on the stage, waving.

Barton Green had slung his camera to one side now and he was talking to Opal. He gestured towards the waiting crowd. It looked as if he was offering her the chance to leave the stage. He had been trying to take her photograph for weeks but he didn't seem to want it any more. Maybe he was letting her go. Maybe she could still get her CIA and return to Carnelia that night after all. It could still be all right.

To Martha's astonishment, Opal was shaking her head. She took Barton Green's hand and shook it vigorously. Then she arranged herself on a barrel, with the treasure chest on her lap, lifted her sunglasses and posed.

Barton seemed taken aback. Martha knew the eyes behind the sunglasses weren't the huge alien ones he'd been expecting to see. He looked a bit lost for a moment but then Opal nodded at him in a reassuring sort of way and he took a few slow steps backwards, raised the camera and snapped.

The flash from the camera was greeted by a far greater flash from Opal's eyes. It zapped madly, jaggedly to and fro like low level lightning, and then disintegrated into a mass of violet particles which flew upwards, a vast school of radiant flying fish, and then curved over and rained down on the crowd in a billion twinkling droplets.

There was a short and quite terrible silence. No one seemed to know what had happened. The crowd was stunned. Martha and Robbie exchanged horrified glances. Uncle Bixbite and Opal's eyes met and locked together. They appeared to be carrying on an intense and very fierce psychic conversation.

The silence was broken by a tremendous explosion which made everyone jump with shock. Then the first rocket hit the sky and showered down in silver and gold. Another rocket went up. Then another, and another until the night was ricocheting with pops and bangs and the sky was studded with a million multi-coloured lights.

Martha studied the upturned faces around her, all staring at the fireworks display with rapt attention. None of them had guessed the truth. They all thought the light that had sprung from Opal's eyes had simply been the first firework. She knew, of course. So did Robbie, so did Barton Green. So did Uncle Bixbite. He broke off his silent conversation with Opal, pulled his bat mingle from his ear and stuffed it, still upside down, in his breast pocket. Then he stormed off, barging through the crowd and up the steps of a temporary toilet.

Looking back at Opal, Martha saw that she was looking at her too. She wasn't running after Uncle Bixbite, trying to persuade him to change his mind. She wasn't watching the fireworks. She was just sitting very calmly on the barrel and smiling her broad smile. Then, slowly, she raised a hand and beckoned.

Opal Moonbaby wasn't going back to Carnelia after all. She was staying put.

Feeling as if she was in a dream, a dream she never wanted to end, Martha began to press her way through the crowd towards the stage. Towards her friend.

Last of all . . .

B arton Green sits on the sofa in the head office of Pirate Planet. He has his arm round Polly Pringle, who is leaning contentedly on his shoulder, her eyes closed. Polly's office is the highest thing in the whole place, even higher than the Terror of the High Seas roller coaster. It has floor-to-ceiling windows. You can see everything from up here. Things that other people, people on the ground, would never notice. They're all down there, milling around, hardly bigger than ants. Not one of them has noticed the silver toilet cubicle whizzing through the night sky like an angry egg. It's almost out of sight now, hardly distinguishable from one of those twinkling faraway stars.

And if anyone looked up now, they wouldn't be able to see the faces of the two girls on the roller coaster. There they are, strapping themselves in. Barton recognises them both. One is short with pink cheeks

and cropped dark hair. The other is tall, gangly and pale, her hair so light it's almost white. They couldn't be more different. One thing about them is the same though. It's the look of bliss on their faces as the wagon they are in begins to move. They cling together, squealing and laughing as they zoom down the roller coaster track, the pale girl's hair streaming out behind them, luminous as the moon against the black sky.

Barton Green smiles. Humming to himself, he looks down at his camera, at a photo he has taken earlier in the evening. It's a brilliant photo, his best ever. It could probably make him famous, change his life. Look at those eyes! Astonishing! People would pay good money for that photo. It's a work of art. People would see it and wonder how he did it. If he showed it to them at the milk depot they'd have to eat their words, all those rotten things they'd said about him. If they saw this, they'd think he was one cool guy.

Polly stirs next to him. She looks so pretty, asleep like that. Even her gentle snoring sounds pretty to Barton. He shifts a little to make her more comfortable.

He looks back at the photo, just one more time. After all, what does he care for money? What does he care *what* people think of him? He doesn't care at all. Not any more. He strokes Polly's cheek, traces the line of her top lip with his index finger. Fame? Fortune? He doesn't need all that. He already has everything he needs, right here.

Barton goes through the camera's menu until he finds the button he is looking for. The *DELETE* button.

He presses it and the photo vanishes.

201

Acknowledgements

This first book comes with many thanks to the following people:

Jo Unwin, my friend and agent, for her encouragement, insight and support, and to the great team at Conville & Walsh; Fiona Kennedy and all at Orion, particularly Jenny Glencross for her wise and sympathetic editing, and Nina Douglas and Louise Court for spreading the word; Gillian Johnson for bringing Opal zinging so vibrantly onto the page; Julia Green, Steve Voake, Nicola Davies and all who have worked with me, tutors and students alike, at Bath Spa University. Love and thanks to my husband and fellow writer, Gary Parker, for being so sure I could do it; and our girls, Madeleine and Emma, for insisting on being read to every single night.

Thank you!